AMY REDEK

Discoveries In College

Brooke LIKES IT SOFT

Intense and Sexy Bisexual Erotica

WARNING

This book contains sexually explicit scenes and adult language. It may be considered offensive to some readers. This book is for sale to adults ONLY.

Please store your files wisely where they cannot be accessed by underage readers.

* * * * * * * * * * * * * * * * * * *

WANT FREE COPIES OF MY BOOKS?
Just visit my blog and download free copies of my books:
amy-redek.awesomeauthors.org/amy-redek

About the Publisher

4Fun Publishing, a member of **BLVNP Incorporated**, 340 S. Lemon #6200, Walnut CA 91789, info@blvnp.com / legal@blvnp.com
NOTE: Due to the highly emotional reaction of some people to works of erotic fiction, any email sent to the above address that contains foul language or religious references is automatically deleted by our anti-spam software and will not be seen. All other communications are welcome.

DISCLAIMER

Please don't be stupid and kill yourself. This book is a work of FICTION. Do not try any new sexual practice that you find in this book. It is fiction and not to be confused with reality. Neither the author nor the publisher or its associates assume any responsibility for any loss, injury, death or legal consequences resulting from acting on the contents in this book. Every character in this book is over 18 years of age. The author's opinions are not to be construed as the opinions of the publisher. The material in this book is for entertainment purposes ONLY. Enjoy.

Brooke Likes It Soft

Discoveries in College
Intense and Sexy Bisexual Erotica

By: Amy Redek

© Amy Redek 2015
ISBN: 978-1-68030-526-5

(This book is dedicated to Myra)

It's difficult to know where to start, to tell you how I came to be a lesbian. It's not that I don't like men, I do, but given the choice between sex with a man or a woman, the latter comes first. I like that, 'comes first', for I've only got to see a woman or girl that catches my eye and I'm coming before I've even spoken to her. Many's the time that I've wet my panties and had the fluid running down on the inside of my thighs at just the thought of what they would be like in bed. Mind you, a bed's not always been the place to have sex I can tell you. And I will as we go along through the years until we reached where I am now.

If just this opening is beginning to titillate you, oh, there I go again. Anything to do with tits and I'm on my way to the head of the queue to sample them. By that I mean that I love to stroke them, to gently mould them in the palm of my hand. To feel the nipple rise up to be a hard little bud that just begs to be sucked, tongued and nibbled. To me that is titillating. But it's not only the tits that I love, it's the whole lovely silken body of a female that I like to run my hands over. Running my fingers through a luxuriant head of hair to bring my hands down to smooth cheeks that I can pull towards my face for me to kiss them before moving to the lips.

The first kiss is one that you never forget. The softness of the lips, the slight moisture you can feel as they meet. That first one is always a gentle brushing of them that sends a tingle all down the spine and creates a warm glow right inside. Your hands then slowly leave the cheeks and move slowly down the other's back so that you can pull them closer to your own body, the pressure of the lips increasing as your bodies meld together, feeling the breasts that you've admired and can now feel pressing up against yours. Even now my body is trembling as it does at that first bodily contact, the kissing becoming more intensified as the lips start to part and you can feel the teeth and then the tongue of the one you are kissing.

God, I'm soaking wet already in telling you this, for this is just the start. I'm sitting here in the college library writing this and sitting opposite my bed mate, Aleena. I say bed mate for we both sleep together in either bed of our four bed room, the other two being Sammy and Elaine, all four of us love having female sex with the other two sharing a bed at night as we did. Aleena has just looked up from what she's reading and has given me that smile again that drives me wild and it makes me want to drag her off to our room where we can fuck each other.

My heart is pounding and making me lose track of what I'm trying to do, and that is write the story of my life so far, leading up to where I am now, sitting down and trying to write. Damn the girl with that smile, making me squeeze my thighs together and not think of her between them as she used her mouth and tongue to bring me up to an orgasm. It's taking me a great deal of effort to stay seated and forcing the images of us in bed as we would caress each other's breasts before sucking on them and nibbling away at the hard nipples that have been aroused.

Stop it! One half of my mind is screaming out at the other half, to concentrate on what you've set out to do. It is sheer will power that makes me bend my head to carry on with what I've started. Take deep breaths and get the heart to stop pounding, I said to myself as I picked up my pen again and bent myself to the self-imposed task I had set myself and begin to write.

My first few years of my life are hazy as would be expected, not really knowing much till I was around four years old. It was a small apartment that I lived in with my mom, not ever knowing my father for he died when I was two, so my ma told me. He had worked for a construction company and had been seeing to the cables being set in a new underground train network when the roof collapsed, killing him and two other men. Fortunately the company was Government sponsored and so he was insured by them which was a God send to us and at the same time, mom was entitled to a widow's pension as well. So our standard of living remained the same, feeding and clothing us though ma still worked as a manageress in a dress boutique.

When I was born, mom obviously had taken maternity leave for six months and her job was held open for her. Now all this is what she told me later, and ongoing back to run the shop, took me with her, setting up a small playpen in the store room where I had to stay while she ran the shop. It was because of her position that she could do this and as I grew up and began to walk, she also used me as a model for children's clothes to show to prospective buyers. It wasn't a cheap shop and the clothes were only for the rich.

I got to like dressing up in these expensive clothes and showing them off and didn't mind when a hand was run over my body as the buyer checked out the quality. It gave me a queer feeling at having a woman's hand run over me even though I was dressed. This feeling intensified as I grew older and didn't object when a hand also began to move over some bared flesh when being dressed up.

It was around this time with me being now four years old that mom got married again and so I now had a step-father that was good for both of us (I think). He had a good job with a computer company and so we had enough money to live quite comfortable and moved into a bigger house.

On growing up, I would play with the other kids of the neighborhood and also went to school with them, but I liked Saturdays and the holidays for I would then be in the shop with mom and didn't mind stripping to be naked in front of others there as I was dressed in what they wanted to see.

I was twelve when my breasts started to develop and began to get a light fuzz of hair at my groin as I reached puberty. I loved my growing body and would spend quite some time in my bedroom at night, looking at myself in the wardrobe mirror as I stroked my hands up and down my chest and sides. I would run my hands over my growing breasts and squeeze them and make the nipples stand up like little nuts and would tweak them and get a funny feeling grow inside my stomach as I did so. Years later, I found that I could also get the same thrill by rubbing my fingers in between the thick lips of my sex and found a little bud there that really excited me when I stroked and rubbed it.

So much so that I would also lie on my bed and frig myself and so had my first orgasm that sent me like a rocket to the moon. I was shaking and couldn't stop the way my heels were drumming the bed at the euphoric sensations that flew through my body, making me see rainbows on the ceiling and have a great lassitude of the body as I came down from the dizzy heights that my body had taken me.

I was hooked, just like a drug addict only for me it was frigging myself and not sniffing or injecting drugs into my veins. Every night from then on I would stick my fingers up inside my sex and work my clit as I got to know what it was called as well as my vagina. This I would do but knew that something was missing as I kept using my fingers up inside me and suddenly found an answer one day when I was in the kitchen. It was a large knobbly cucumber.

This I smuggled up to my bedroom and quickly got my clothes off and lay on the bed and gave the cucumber a kiss before putting it between my legs and slowly started to push it into my vagina. I used my left hand to do this and used the fingers on the other hand to play with my clit, rubbing and nipping it between my fingers as the cucumber slowly moved up into me.

I could feel all the knobbly bits on the outer skin until it seemed to be blocked, so I gave it an extra shove and had a sudden pain as it suddenly moved right into me. It was later that I found that I had broken through my hymen which was a sign of a virgin when intact. But the pain was only a sharp one that didn't linger as my body began to become aroused at having this thick cucumber being moved inside me. It created more sensations as I twisted it inside as I moved it back and forth as I worked my clit.

It was ecstasy! Using that cucumber and my fingers at the same time until, with great pleasure, would explode with an orgasm that seemed to get better every time I had one. I would use one nearly every time I wanted to play with myself, even in the bathroom. It was in there one day when I got caught using it.

Our bathroom wasn't a big one. As you went in, the bath was facing you and off to the left of the door was the washbasin and between the bath and the basin was the toilet pan. I found that with the toilet pan cover down, I could sit on it and lean back against the wall and have my feet on the side of the bath with my legs open and could use the cucumber.

I was in there one day and I'd just had a bath and was now sitting on the pan, still naked and had the cucumber suck up inside me as I frigged myself, leaning back against the wall with my eyes closed and never heard the door open.

'Well I wondered where the cucumbers kept disappearing to,' I heard my mom speak. I nearly shat myself as my eyes flew open and saw her standing there, looking down at me, my fingers inside me as well as the latest cucumber. I couldn't read the expression on her face or her eyes as she looked at my naked body with me frozen like a statue at having been found doing what I was doing.

'Well, my little girl is becoming a woman so I think it's about time that we had a talk later. Now get off the pan and to bed, I want a pee.'

Well I'd never been so embarrassed in my life as I was then, getting caught in the act by my mom and seeing me naked like I was and with what I was doing to myself. I'm sure my face was bright red as I pulled out my pleasure toy and got up off the seat and quickly ran past her and out of the bathroom and into my bedroom. I flung myself on the bed, throwing the cucumber to one side as I cried into my pillow, cursing myself for getting caught like that. What must she be thinking of me?

It wasn't long before mom came into my room and sat down on the bed next to me. She sat there for nearly an hour telling me that it was normal for a young girl as myself to find out about herself in this way. She sat there for nearly an hour telling me that a young girl should be told all from menstruation, the ovulation period, right through to having male sex. Stressing the fact that if and when, this last said with a smile, that I should always make sure that the boy or man wore a condom. In fact she was very liberal in what she said and didn't chastise me at all for what I had been doing and with her not saying anything about the cucumber for which I was thankful.

I got a surprise two days later when dad, that's what I called him even if he wasn't my real father, came home earlier than usual and told me to follow him into his office. I had been sitting at the dining table doing my homework when he said this. Oh shit, I thought to myself, what's he going to say, for he only ever asked me in there when he wanted to give me a telling off? So with a little trepidation, I closed my book and followed him into his office as he called it. He went and sat down behind his desk and told me to sit down on the couch that was in front of it. I was wearing my sundress then and smoothed out the back as I sat down to face him.

'Well, Brooke, your mom told me that she found you in the bathroom, playing with yourself and using a cucumber.' I felt my face going all red with him saying this. 'And that she had a few words with you about sex and to be careful when you might find yourself alone with a boy. Well I've gone and bought you something that might keep you away from them until you're old enough,' he said and turned round to his filing cabinet and opened one of the drawers and pulls out a bag and emptied the contents on his desk. It was three sex toys. One was like a rabbit with ears and pearls, another was of an erect male penis and the third a thong with, in the crotch it had a tiny vibrator. This when wearing it, the vibrator would be tight up to the clit and when turned on, really excited the clit and it could be used anywhere. Sitting in the class room, on a bus, anywhere, and by just feeling down could press the button to set it working. Boy, it's fucking hard not to scream out when it brings you up to an orgasm. This one I did get round to using later.

'I'm not going to punish you but I need to make sure that you know how to use these safely.' He picked up the penis one and got up from behind his desk and came round and handed it to me before then sitting on the edge of his desk. I looked at it wide eyed and looked up at him with a question in my eyes. 'You should use that instead of a cucumber,' giving out a chuckle. 'Using this should keep you away from the boys.' I looked at it a bit more closely, holding this fake male penis in my hand, never having seen one of these before, real or rubber, and didn't know that it was like a male that had been circumcised. I moved it around in my hand, feeling it soft in part but having a solid feeling to it in the middle. 'Turn it over,' he said, which I did so.

'It's called a vibrator, see that knob at the base? Give it a twist.' This I did and felt the damn thing seem to come to life, throbbing away in my hand and smiled at the feeling of it in my hand and then noticed that it had a small hard knob at the base below the shaft and wondered what that was there for, but found out a few minutes later.

'Th…thank you, Dad,' I stuttered, almost certain that my face was red with him knowing what it was for.

'Now I want you to use it, here, now, in front of me,' he said, still sitting there in front of me. I was stunned at what he had said and I'm sure that he was enjoying my discomfort at what he had told me to do.

'I…I can't,' I stammered, my heart thumping away in my chest. 'You will,' he said with a grim look on his face. 'You use it now in front of me or you will be grounded until you do.'

It was a Catch-22 situation. If I didn't do as he said, I would be grounded and if I did, he would then see my pussy. I had no choice and had a queer thrill run through my body and I felt myself starting to get wet between my thighs at the thought of him watching as I used this toy penis. Well I didn't mind showing my body off at the shop, in fact, I rather liked being naked and having people look at me, though they had always been women. Now I was being asked to show myself to a man for the first time, that man being my dad. In fact, that little thrill was getting bigger all the time at the thought. So with a shrug of my shoulders, put that toy cock down and stood up and pulled my sundress up over my head and sat back down naked and picked up this rubberized penis and wondered if it would fit. But the cucumber did and this was a bit smaller.

I put my fingers down between my legs and felt that some of my juices had made me very wet and slowly began to push the head of this cock up into my pussy. I looked up to see that dad had a big smile on his face, watching as I pushed it right up inside me and then found that the little knob that I'd noticed earlier, sat right up against my clit. It felt quite comfortable inside and gave the bottom a twist and nearly jumped out of my skin as it began to vibrate inside me.

Oh bloody fucking hell! Having this cock throb and pulsate away inside me and the extra pleasure of feeling it excite my clit didn't take me long to lean back and begin to shake as my orgasm wasn't far off and my whole body went rigid as my insides seemed to explode and felt it starting to pour out of me. I was in heaven at the joy and pleasure of having such a massive orgasm and didn't care now that dad had been watching me go through the throes of excitement.

I came down from that height of ecstasy to see dad's grinning face as I began to pull that false cock out of my cunt.

'Now let me see you suck on it,' he said.

'Suck on it?' I cried out, looking at this cock in my hand, all shiny with my juices.

'Yes. Get to know what you taste like. Go on, suck it!'

I looked at the shiny head and slowly lifted it up, feeling my juices on the shaft and had my tongue run round my lips as I then opened them and took the head of this cock into my mouth. It was wet, just like my pussy, as I began to suck up my own orgasmic fluid. It wasn't too bad either and finished up running my tongue all round it, savoring the taste that wasn't unpleasant and would have liked to taste some more, but it was all clean now. I gave dad a triumphant smile as I put it to one side and picked my dress up and pulled it over my head, standing up to smooth down the front.

'That was good, Brooke. You're not grounded. Now use them instead of going with the boys,' he said as he straightened himself up and I couldn't but help notice that he had a bulge at the front of his trousers.

He quickly moved back round his desk to sit down as I picked up the other two sex toys and with the penis, put them in the bag which I took with me out of his office.

I quickly ran upstairs to my room and when inside with the door shut, quickly took my sundress off and got onto the bed and took this rubber cock out of the bag. It looked huge in my hand and at least eight inches long and quite thick towards the base. I put my fingers down to my pussy and found that I was already dribbling some fluid out of my body at the thought of what was going to be put inside again where my fingers were.

I laid myself back on my pillows, having them half upright so that I could see what I was doing and opened my legs and slowly put it in between my sex lips and felt the head of it touch the entrance to my vagina and gave out a shiver before I began to gently ease it inside me. Being so wet down there in anticipation, it slipped in easily and kept on pushing it inside me until the base was tight up against my body and had that the little knob touching my clit.

It felt comfortable inside me, surprised again that I could take that length inside and I then gave the knob at the base a twist and had it suddenly start to vibrate.

'Christ!' I gasped, for I could feel that little knob rubbing against my clit as well as having the whole thing throbbing away and I nearly had an orgasm there and then, but somehow managed to hold myself back as I lay there, now stroking and rubbing my tits with my hands as this rubber cock pulsated away thrilling me no end. My nipples had risen up too and with the palm of my hand rubbing across them excited me even further and it was only for another minute or two before I had to bring my thighs tight together, keeping this cock inside me as I began to shake and shudder and had to bite my hand to stop myself screaming out as I came with one almighty orgasm.

The orgasm came to a stop but my body still kept on shaking as the vibrator kept grinding away inside my pussy, my chest was heaving as

I panted away and it took another couple of minutes before I got myself under control. I opened my legs and reached down and turned it off and slowly pulled it out. I couldn't stop my inside muscle from flexing themselves round the shaft as if to try and keep it there inside me, but out it came with a loud sucking noise.

I rolled over with it in my hand and looked at the head, glistening with my juices and had the sudden urge to suck it. I opened my mouth and took in as much as I could, getting the second taste of my orgasmic juices. I sucked and slobbered over this wonderful toy and knew that this from now on was my best friend. I sucked on the head of this cock and even gently chewed it until it was all clean and then lifted my head and used my tongue to lick all round the shaft and base to get the rest of my coming off of it.

I rolled over onto my back and began to rub it between my tits and all over my stomach and lower chest before sucking on it again. 'I'm going to call you my Peter,' I whispered to it before poking my tongue into the small slit at the top, knowing that it would not be long before I had it back up inside me. I was right for it wasn't long before I had Peter back up inside to drive me wild with another orgasm, thrashing about on the bed as my whole body seemed to be charged with electricity as many nerves kept vibrating in time to Peter's pulsating throb. I've still got Peter along with quite a few other sex toys that dad bought me having to show him how I used each one.

I now always began having that tingle run up and down my spine when he presented me with a new one, knowing that he would get to see my naked body, my tits getting bigger all the time. I know he got a thrill too for he always seemed to be hard inside his trousers as he watched me use the new toy inside me.

The only problem I found with the thong vibrator that he had given me was that I then had to wear a pad too to catch and absorb my orgasmic juices that had flowed out of me for I felt most embarrassed the first time that these fluids ran down my inner thigh.

It was thirteen bit later when I had a real live cock put up inside me instead of me using Peter, and that cocks man was my Uncle Stevie and married to Auntie Mischelle. Though I called them uncle and auntie, they were not related to us but friends of mom, well Auntie was. I was told that with a child like myself, it wasn't the proper thing to do to call adults by their Christian names. So I had to use the prefix uncle and auntie whenever I spoke to them. They would come round to our house quite often as mom and I would go to theirs though dad seldom came with us, preferring to work on one of his computer programs.

I remember it was summertime and the air was quite sultry and because of this humid heat, wore a half top, shorts and sandals. My breasts had been growing at an alarming rate and were now quite prominent when wearing this top. They weren't quite big enough for me to wear a bra though I did have one but didn't like wearing it, as to me, it felt quite restrictive.

Mom never said anything about me not wearing this bra and dad never noticed when we said goodbye to him that day as he was concentrating on what he was doing with his computer. It wasn't far to walk to my 'Aunt' and 'Uncle's' home and we soon got inside and found it was just as hot inside as it was outside as they didn't have an air conditioner as we did.

We had a light lunch as they talked and it's only on reflection that Uncle Stevie kept looking at me more often than he used to, but I didn't notice this at the time. With our meal over, mom and Auntie had been talking about going out to the shops and did we, that is Uncle Stevie and myself, want to go with them?

'No,' said Uncle, 'I'll stay here. It's too hot to be walking about while you look at things that you're not going to buy. I need a shower to cool me down. Brooke can stay and keep me company and help me do the dishes.'

To be quite frank, I didn't really want to go anyway and so I nodded in agreement, not knowing what was going to happen that afternoon. So mom and Auntie went off after saying that they would be out for a couple of hours and Uncle and I gathered up the dishes and he washed them up while I dried them before putting them away. This didn't take long and we were soon finished and he said he was going for his shower.

He went off to his bedroom that had its own bathroom just off the room while I sat and looked through a magazine that was on the coffee table in the living room. He came out of the bedroom about fifteen minutes later wearing a white terrycloth robe and sat down in front of me.

'Would you rather have gone out with them?' he asked me.

'No,' I replied, putting the magazine down. 'It's too hot outside today, besides, it's too boring just walking about the Mall.'

'Would you like a cool glass of wine?' he asked.

'Ooh yes please,' I said eagerly, feeling quite grown up at being asked if I wanted a drink that I would never be allowed to have at home.

'Well there's an open bottle in the fridge. Pour out two big glasses for the both of us,' he said sitting back in the chair. I got up and went off to the kitchen and got the glasses out and the wine from the fridge, and pouring some out into the glasses before putting the bottle back and taking the glasses back through to the living room. Walking back inside and towards him, I noticed that the front of his robe had come undone and his cock was sticking straight out from between the folds. I pretended not to notice this as I handed him a glass and went and sat back down myself and looked at his cock sticking up like it was and it looked as if it was bigger than Peter.

'Uncle,' I said after taking a sip of wine. 'The front of your robe is undone at the front and you are sticking out.'

He looked down at it and gave me a grin. 'You're right,' he said, not bothering to cover himself. 'The bloody thing always does that after having a hot shower. It's as if it is trying to cool down. Tell you what, if you don't mind me sitting here with it sticking out, I'll give you $10, and it will be our secret and enjoy your glass of wine.'

I know now that it was not only a bribe but also a reference that I was drinking wine which I was not supposed to have and him saying that it would be our secret.

I had never had wine before and it was pleasant to drink and made feel kind of relaxed and calm.

'For ten dollars, you can sit anyway you like,' and wondered why I had said that for he then opened his legs and the action pulled the robe open wide and I had his erect cock fully out in the open, for me to look at it. It fascinated me to see it twitch occasionally, lifting up and settling back down, staring at me and I could see the little slit on the head that appeared to wink at me when it did this.

'Is this the first time you've seen a man's cock?' he asked, having noticed where my eyes were looking.

'Er, yes,' I said.

'It's bigger than most men's as you'll find out later in life,' he said, 'and it's at least nine inches long, if not ten when fully hard.'

'I don't believe that it's that long,' I said.

'I tell you what. Go into your Auntie's room and look in her sewing drawer. There's a measuring tape there. Bring it back and I'll show you.'

I put my glass down and went off to the room, found the tape and brought it back to where he was sitting and offered it to him.

'It's quite hard to measure it yourself correctly,' he said, sitting up and moving his body to the edge of the chair, his cock giving a slight up and down movement. 'I'll give you another $10 if you do the measuring.'

Now twenty dollars was a lot of money to me and nobody would ever know, so I knelt down between his legs and start to measure him. I held one end of the tape against his pubic hair, up against his stomach and ran the tape along the shaft of his cock till it reached the head of his cock. I had to bend my head it then being only a couple of inches from looking down at the head of it. My fingers were actually touching a man's real live cock and I had this tingle run and down my spine at the contact.

'Seven inches!' I exclaimed 'There! I said it wasn't as long as nine inches.'

'Well you have to play with it a bit to reach the nine inches. Tell you what. I'll give you another $10 if you stroke it with your hand a few times and if does not get any bigger, I'll give you another ten.'

Wow, I said to myself. If it doesn't grow any bigger that will be forty dollars. Now that was a small fortune to me then and so I took his cock into my hand, feel the heat of it as well as it throbbing away. It was a much different feeling than holding Peter as it vibrated to having this real pulsating cock in my hand.

'Well, rub it then. Hold it tight too,' he said. So I began moving my hand, feeling the soft silky skin move so smoothly over the solid flesh that it covered.

'Harder,' he said again. 'Harder.' I then realized that the wine had got to me having his cock in my hand and rubbing it harder and harder. After a minute or two he spoke again.

'Measure it now.' So I let go of it, rather reluctantly really and picked up the tape and measured it again and found that it had only increased an inch.

'Eight inches. That's it,' I said quite proudly that it had just cost him another ten dollars.

'Okay. You win. But it does reach nine inches when it's fully hard. Your Auntie can make it grow to that length. She puts it into her mouth and sucks on it. Tell you what, I'll give you another twenty dollars if you suck on it as she does.'

'That would make it sixty dollars,' I said, and my voice must have sounded a little petulant as I looked down at his throbbing erection, wondering if it would fit in my mouth. He must have interpreted the way that I had spoken and with my head down that I was reluctant to suck on him, which I really did want to do this to see if it was better than sucking on Peter.

'I'll make it a round hundred then if you will do it,' he said. I looked up to see an expectant expression on his face. I gave him a smile.

'Okay,' I said and his face lit up and he gave me a big smile as I bent my head and gave the head of his cock a lick, taking in a little pearl of fluid that was in the eye of his cock with my tongue and found it very sweet to the taste. I pulled the foreskin down and licked all round the bared flesh and felt his body give out a shiver as I was resting my arms on his outspread legs. I then ran my tongue right down the underside of his shaft and back up.

'Don't forget my balls,' he said in a strangled voice. I looked up and saw that his body was quite rigid and gave him a smile and bent back down and licked his balls and even took each one into my mouth and moved that soft plum around being careful to not suck it too hard. On letting them go, licked my way back up the shaft and finally took as much of his cock into my mouth as I could without having it choke me. I started off slowly but as I got used to sucking on him I began to move my head up and down a bit faster as I did with my hand.

But then I had trouble, for he put both hands to my head and began pushing me down harder onto his big cock. I tried to lift my head up but he kept on pushing it down as he spoke.

'That's it, cocksucker! Suck on it, you slut! That…that's great,' he gasped, calling me names as he still kept pushing my head down onto him, making me being fucked in the mouth. The next thing I knew was that having his cock so deep in my mouth, it began to enter my throat making me gag. Not only did he keep trying to force it even further into my throat, I could feel some of his pre-cum leaking out of his cock and it sliding down my throat making me want to cough.

'That's right. Keep sucking, I'm nearly there. I'm going to cum in that lovely mouth you've got, you slut. You're a nice cocksucker,' and he gave out a groan and I felt the head of his cock swell a little more and his cock started to shoot out his cum, flooding my mouth with it. Not once, but six fucking times his cum kept adding more to that first shot until there wasn't any room left and started to have some of it come out the side of my mouth and run down my chin. 'Swallow it! Swallow it, you cocksucker,' and slowly eased himself back a little, still keeping the head in my mouth but carried on holding my head.

With him easing back a little I was then able to do as he said and so for the first time, I swallowed, or rather gulped a man's cum down into my throat to slide down into my stomach. He held my head until I'd finished swallowing it before he pulled his cock right out and I could see that it might just be nine inches as he said it would get with it being sucked.

'Show me your tongue now,' he said as he took hold of his still big and throbbing cock. I stuck my tongue out and had him hit it gently with the head of his cock, shaking out the last of his cum out of the end of it. 'Now swallow that as well,' which I did and found that it wasn't that bad in the taste, maybe just a trifle salty, but not bad otherwise. 'Okay. You can get up now,' he said with a big smile on his face, 'and can go in the bathroom and wash out your mouth. You can bring me back my pants too.'

I got up off my knees and went into the bathroom and stood by the basin in front of the mirror and gave myself a smile, for I confess that I actually enjoyed sucking on him and just loved the taste of his cum. I ran my tongue round inside my mouth, still having the taste of him inside and so I just ran the water into the basin but didn't wash out my mouth as he said. I gave another smile to the mirror before leaving the bathroom and picking up his pants to take back into the living room. I passed his pants over to him and he took them and put his hand into one of the pockets and brought some money and pulled out two new fifty dollar bills and put them in my hand.

'Now don't forget. This is our little secret,' and gave me a grin. 'Maybe we can do this again some time.'

'Maybe we can, Uncle Stevie,' I said back with a smile and impulsively, leaned over him and kissed him and somehow, my tongue went in between his lips and teeth and ran my tongue round his. It was a long kiss and both of us panted for breath when I pulled my head back. He had a strange look on his face as he sat there looking at me, his tongue slowly moving round over his lips.

'Did you wash out your mouth?' he asked.

'Of course I did, Uncle. You told me too so I did,' I lied.

'Well, I'd better get dressed before your mom and your aunt get back, oh,' he said as he got up from the chair. 'Wash those glasses up. We can't have them knowing that I gave you a drink.' This was said with a smirk with his innuendo what with me not only having had a glass of wine to drink, but drank his cum too. So he went off to the bedroom to get dressed while I took the glasses into the kitchen quite happy at getting a hundred dollars from him for what I thought was a most pleasurable half hour in licking and sucking his cock and didn't even mind being called a slut and a cocksucker.

He came back into the sitting room fully dressed with a smug smile on his face and sat down opposite me.

'How about us having a cup of coffee?' he asked, picking up a magazine.

'Okay,' I said, getting and throwing my magazine of the coffee table and went off to the kitchen. I had the kettle on when both mom and auntie arrived back from the mall and both came into the kitchen.

'Oh Brooke dear,' said mom. 'Are you making coffee?' I gave her a nod. 'Lovely. We're both dying for a cup, aren't we, Mischelle?'

'We certainly are', she replied, coming over to take over the job of making the coffee. So with coffee cups on the kitchen table, Uncle Stevie had his in the living room, it was small talk about what shops they went into while in the mall. It wasn't long after finishing our coffee that mom and I said our goodbyes and got a wink from Uncle Stevie, with him putting a finger to his lips behind the other two backs. I nodded my acknowledgement and fingered the two bills in the pocket of my sundress.

A month later they both came to our house and both mom and Auntie Mischelle went off to the Mall again, but dad was at home, so Uncle Stevie could only give me a wry smile and a shake of his head as he licked his lips. I unconsciously gave mine a lick too before I realized what I was implying by that action and soon stopped.

Another month passed before we went off to their house again. Only this time I was wearing a tank top and a pair of shorts and got a kiss on the cheek from Uncle Stevie this time.

'You won't be going off to the Mall with them, will you?' he asked when we were left alone in the living room, his eyes almost pleading.

'No,' I said, giving him a smile which made him smile too.

So mom and Auntie Mischelle went off to the mall again leaving me with Uncle Stevie. It was him this time that went out to the kitchen and came back with two large glasses of chilled wine and came and sat down next to me and handed me a glass. Nothing was said as he pulled a hand out of his trouser pocket and put three fifty dollar bills on the coffee table before turning to me and clinking his glass against mine.

'You seem to be growing up fast, Brooke,' he said as his hand came up and had the palm of his hand run over the tit nearest to him. Well just that action made the nipple rise up instantly and he obviously felt it harden under his touch.

'These seem to be getting bigger every time I see you. You don't mind me touching them, do you?' he asked, his hand still moving gentle over this tit.

'No,' I said softly, liking that touch and the warm feeling I was getting in my stomach though more of a glow like a lit candle, looking at those three bills on the coffee table.

'Can I see them?' he asked, his hand moving down to stroke across my bare stomach making that glow get warmer and warmer. I nodded and he turned slightly, his hand coming off me and with both hands, pulled my top up and right over my head so that I was then completely bare up top. 'Wonderful,' he breathed, his head moving closer to my body. 'So wonderful that they look as though they are waiting to be kissed. Would you like me to kiss them?'

I didn't notice the gleam in his eye as he looked at me for my answer. It was a look that I was to see often in other men's eyes as they looked at my body later on when they were much bigger.

When I had played with my tits before, making the nipples rise up to be hard little nodules, I had wished that if only I could have sucked on them myself and so I nodded for him to kiss and suck them. His head came down to the tit nearest him and had my body tremble as his mouth closed over the nipple and felt him suck on it. The glow in my stomach was now a fire and I couldn't help but give out a groan, especially when I felt his teeth gently nibble the one in his mouth. His hand hadn't been idle for that was now on my other tit and giving it a gentle rub making that nipple rise up as hard as the one that was in his mouth.

I could feel the suction as he sucked after that nibble, his tongue now making me squirm a little on the sofa as I felt myself getting wet between my thighs and couldn't stop my hand from giving myself a rub there. He must have seen what my hand was doing as he sucked on me, for his hand came and took mine and placed it on his trouser front. His cock was hard inside and he rubbed my hand over it and I got another thrill inside me at feeling his hard cock again.

'Oh Brooke,' he moaned as he tried to shift his lower body to make himself more comfortable. 'You don't know what you are doing to me,' his mouth briefly off my nipple to utter these soft words, and felt his hand move and heard the zipper of his trousers being pulled down. His hand then took mine again and pushed inside his trousers. He wasn't wearing shorts and my fingers came in contact for the second time with his hard penis, though cock should be the right word with it being so big and hard.

My fingers curled round it and with him moving slightly again, it came out from his trousers with my fingers still round that hard flesh and now it was in my hand and I could feel it throbbing away, just like my heart was at doing this. The fire in my belly was now a raging inferno at having a real live Peter in my hand, feeling that soft silky skin move so easily over the hard flesh that it covered.

A feeling that I didn't have when my hand rubbed my Peter. This was much better and had the sudden urge to suck his hard cock again and moved my head and looked down at what I was holding and wasn't surprised to see that the head of his cock had the foreskin stretched tight round the red and hot glowing flesh.

The eye of his cock seemed to wink at me as I squeezed it just below the head and wanted to put my tongue inside it. He must have read my mind.

'Would you like to suck on it again as I had sucked on your nipple,' he asked in a strangled voice, having lifted his head up from my tit and looked at me.

'Yes, Uncle,' I said, my voice sounding really thick in my throat, and he leaned up and lay back as I slipped off the sofa, and still holding that pulsating cock in my hand, moved round on my knees and got between his legs and looked at it again. Hard and upright in my hand and looking the same when I saw it two months ago, knowing that it would be able to fit in my mouth. I could see a pearly drop of fluid coming out of the eye and bent my head as I leaned into him and took this off with my tongue.

How sweet was the taste of this clear shining pearl. Sweeter than honey and gave the cock another squeeze and had another drop exude which I licked off again. He gave out a groan at this and then another one as I took the whole head of his cock into my mouth, my lips pushing that skin covering the head down, now knowing that it's called the foreskin. It was hot and could feel it throbbing in time to his heart beat as I held it there for a moment before moving my head up and down as I began to suck him.

God, I'm getting all wet again as I'm writing this, nearly as wet as I was then, remembering that first time I sucked on a man's rampant cock. I think that Aleena would just love to have had my panties now to suck off the juices that are collecting in the gusset of the crotch.

So here I was, sucking my Uncle's cock making his body quiver when my tongue moved over that self heating cock head and found that it was better than sucking Peter.

'Oh Brooke,' he groaned, and I felt him move and he lifted my head up off his cock head and leaned down and kissed me on the mouth. 'Oh Brooke,' he breathed through my lips. 'Let me put it inside you.' Now I really began to soak my thighs for I found that I did want him inside me, throbbing and vibrating as Peter did. He must have seen something in my eyes that must have said yes, for he helped me stand up and didn't stop him from pulling my shorts down and had him bury his face into my pubic hairs that was now a nice soft bush having grown as much as my tits had.

He slipped off the sofa and was on his knees as his tongue began to weave a pattern through the bush of my pussy and felt his tongue push in between the lips of my sex and felt him hit my clit and it made me jump at the sudden wave of pleasure that ran through my body. With the breaking off our contact there, he pulled me down to the floor where he pulled my shorts free from my ankles and open my legs as I was then lying on my back.

I couldn't see his throbbing cock for he bent down and almost lay completely flat between my legs and had his tongue move again up into my sex and had his tongue once again move over my clit making me groan with the erotic feeling and thrill that I was getting. Not only was his soft but hard tongue, a misnomer if ever there was one, was also flitting in and out of my vagina, giving my all kinds of weird sensations but thrilling at the same time.

But then I felt two fingers being pushed up into my twat. Jesus, almost blasphemy, my mind cried out, I'm being sent to heaven, such was the thrill I got as they slid quite easily up the glide path that my juices had created. To have them move about inside was sheer joy and my legs opened even wider, but was thrilled even more when his mouth came up from sucking on me to have his thumb come onto my clit to rub it as his fingers moved inside me, his mouth and tongue licking and sucking on my belly as he moved his body up over mine.

I could feel the fabric of his trouser front rubbing the inside of my thighs and gave out a gasp and shiver as I felt the head of his cock pass the portals of my gate and have him slide himself up into me. My juices helped him slide in without any problem and I felt every inch of him as he widened my inner passage with his throbbing cock. My internal muscles, without me making them do anything, were flexing themselves like mad at this intrusion, trying to grasp the slippery piece of male meat that was invading unknown territory.

My legs went up to grip his waist as I felt his trouser front press up to my groin and had his throbbing cock in as far as it could go before he lifted himself up off my chest to support himself on his forearms. He smiled down at me as I felt his cock twitching inside me, driving me almost wild and he started to move himself before I could say anything about where he was at that moment. Though the words I was going to say were not needed as he was now doing what I wanted, moving his rigid hard cock up and down inside me, scratching and smoothing at the same time, doing what Peter couldn't do to me.

I think it was the sheer delight for him that he was now fucking the daughter of his friend's wife that he didn't last long in the doing of this act, for he was soon grunting with every forceful forward pushing of himself inside me. He suddenly reared up onto fully outstretched arms and really banged his groin into mine as his grunting got louder and came to a halt with just his hips slowly grinding at my pubes but his cock head expanding a little bit more and had him send out his sperm to coat the lining of my inside channel.

Feeling that hot seed suddenly splashing into me made me orgasm and buck like crazy under him as he was shooting up into me, I was sending down my juices for them to collide with his.

There was him humping himself down into me as I was humping myself up to meets his downward thrusts with us both giving out groans at our mutual coming. He had what I would call a sickly grin of his face as we came to a halt, his cock still throbbing away inside me with my muscles there having gone berserk it trying to milk him as they tried to squeeze him even harder.

Both of us were breathing heavily, my chest heaving as much as his was as he slowly lowered himself down till I had his full weight on top of me, his cock still pulsating away inside me. I wasn't at all surprised at him leaning further down and kissing me.

'Thank you, Brooke, thank you,' he said, still trying to get more oxygen into his lungs. 'I've never had better.' What about Auntie, my mind cried out? Didn't he have sex with her? An answer that didn't get answered as it wasn't something that I could ask him. I found out later that the answer, well not quite no, but not far off for she was not only his wife, but wife or husband if you like to another woman for she was a lesbian. This I was to find out later.

He lay on top of me for several minutes and it wasn't until I could feel that his cock was shrinking, shrinking enough to slowly start to slide out of my pussy. My muscles tried to hold him there, but to no avail and I felt it, still hard, after a fashion, finally leave me and with him now out of me, he rolled over onto his back. I rolled onto my side and saw that it still looked fairly hard, lying up on the front of his trousers and wanted to do to it what I did to Peter.

So I moved my body down and lifted up that cock of his, coated in both his sperm and my orgasmic juices and took the head into my mouth as I did with Peter's and sucked not only his cumming but mine too. It was much better having a hot Peter in my mouth than my rubber one and it must have an instinctive reaction on my part, for having him already tonguing my sex, I moved and straddling his upper body so that my sex was right above his face.

As I then sucked on him, I lowered my body and had him licking and sucking me in what is known as the sixty nine position. Now I hadn't heard of this expression before but it just seemed so natural that with me sucking on him, he should be sucking on me.

So after sucking and licking him clean, I moved back round and had him take me in his arms to kiss me with his sticky wet lips and have him thank me for such a wonderful time. That then was the first time that I ever had a rampant cock up inside and have the man who owned it, fuck me. Apart from my Uncle Stevie, there was only one other man that ever fucked me, but we'll come to that later. Strange as it might seem but the best part of us having sex on the floor of his living room, it was his licking and sucking of both my tits and my sex parts that thrilled me the most. I liked the sucking of his cock and of having it up inside me, but it was the licking and the teasing of my clit that was the really best part for me. I was to find out more later at how much I preferred that to being fucked by a man.

That then was my first foray into having sex with a man and finding out, albeit unknowingly which I preferred the most. It wasn't until I had sex with my Auntie did I know where my sexual leanings were going to take me.

It was at school that I found out that quite a few of the older girls were taking birth control pills so that they could have sex but not get pregnant. Knowing this and having the thought of my uncle and myself having sex again gave me a thrill and it was better to be safe than sorry. I did want to have sex with him for I just loved it best when he was down between my thighs licking and using his tongue inside me. So I bought some of these pills from the pharmacy and began taking them.

It was a couple of months later when round at my Auntie's place that mom and her went off shopping again leaving me with Uncle Stevie. It was almost the same as last time though this time, after washing up the lunch things and putting them away, we sat on the sofa and he held my hand.

'Brooke. Did you like what we did last time here?' he asked, giving my hand a little squeeze. I looked down and saw that he had a boner inside his trousers. That was a word I learnt at school that a man's erection was called a boner as well as some other names.

'Yes, Uncle. Especially when you sucked on me,' I said, feeling my face go red at the saying of this.

'Would you like me to do it again?' he asked with a smile.

'Yes please.' So, wearing almost the same clothes as last time, I stood up and quickly took these clothes off and lay down on the carpet as he, this time, took all of his clothes off and now saw my first sight of a man fully naked. His cock was sticking out from the bush of hair that surrounded it and now saw how big his balls were. They looked quite heavy hanging below his rampant cock which swayed from side to side as he went down onto his stomach between my open legs.

His breath was hot as he got close to my pussy and his hands had come up under my legs and over my thighs and felt his fingers part the lips that covered my delicate parts. I couldn't help but give out a shiver, my body trembling as I felt his tongue probe and move all round the inside and then a little jerk as the tip touched my clit. Oh what bliss that was to have his tongue excite me as it moved round and had his face pressed tight up to me as he licked and sucked. I even felt his teeth rasp my clit as it had risen up to be quite hard and this caused the glow in my belly to become a raging fire. Using both teeth and tongue, he licked, sucked and teased this hard little bud of mine, giving me little electric type shocks that built up the passion inside me even more.

I tried to bring my thighs together to hold on to this exquisite experience I was getting, but his head stopped me doing this as my body felt it was being raised up to dizzying heights and felt an orgasm rising up inside me that suddenly exploded. My whole body shook at the incredible pleasure that this was as I felt my outpouring flood down to almost smother him. He'd given out a snort at the first gush of my fluids and then heard the slurping noise as he sucked it into his mouth. His tongue was helping at the same time and I was in heaven at all the sensations that flowed throughout my bucking body.

I was lying there like a lifeless rubber doll when he lifted his head and began kissing my body as he moved up over me and couldn't have stopped him if I had wanted to, I was that lethargic. Besides, he wanted his bit of pleasure too for his own release and I had him push his throbbing cock up into me again for the second time. I got a lot of pleasure at having him move his hard cock inside me though it wasn't as good as having him suck me. My muscles still reacted and constantly moved to try and hold that moving hard flesh as I felt myself building up to another orgasm. He was grunting as he ploughed my almost virgin meadow and with my legs up high, my hands on his shoulders as I began to buck my hips up to the thrusting of his piece of meat into me.

I felt his shoulder muscles start to tighten as he then went quite rigid with his body and only had his hips moving as he tried to ram more of himself up into me, his balls banging against my bum cheeks as he began pumping out his seed. This triggered me off at feeling the sperm hit the walls of my vagina and came myself at the same time giving me that incredible sensation again at having this second orgasm.

He collapsed onto me when he'd finished cumming inside me and I thanked the fact that I was now taking the pill. He squashed my still expanding breasts as he kissed me.

'Thank you, Brooke. I needed that,' he gasped, still trying to get more air into his lungs, his hairy chest heaving against me. 'Will you suck on me again?'

'Yes,' I breathed out, me fighting for air too and would like to have his weight lifted up off me. 'And you can eat my pussy at the same time.' This was something else I had heard at school that when somebody is licking and sucking your sex it was known as "eating pussy".

It was to my relief as he rose up and began to pull out, to which I gave out a small cry, for as much as I wanted him up off of me, I had still liked his cock pulsating inside me. He rolled over onto his back, his wet shining cock slapping up against his lower stomach as I too moved, turning round and getting astride of him. I lifted his wet cock up and took the head into my mouth to lick and suck as I lowered my sex down onto his mouth for him to do the same to me.

I sucked out what sperm he had left inside his cock, taking in some of my own juices, which I rather liked the taste off as he slurped away between my legs, exciting me once again at having his tongue probe and tease both my clit and vagina. The best bit was that while sucking on his still hard rampant cock, I had another orgasm and nearly choked the poor sod as it flooded his mouth. Oh what heavenly bliss that was to have had a third orgasm in such a short time. Having the thrill and ecstasy in the process of this happening, my body tingling with delight and knew that this was the best part of having sex.

But he got me back for nearly drowning him for he nearly choked me. With me having my orgasm, he came and flooded my mouth with his semen, it hitting the back of my throat and gullet. I coughed and nearly lost it and then had more and more come into my mouth as his prick throbbed with every spurt. In a way I was glad when his balls were empty and I was then able to swallow it all in one big go, having it slide down my throat but left enough behind for me to really get the taste of it.

I finished off by licking all over the head of his cock and ran my tongue up and down the shaft to clean it of my own juices and seeing his balls just below my nose, bent that little bit more forward and took one into my mouth and moved it around with my tongue making him give out a groan. I lifted up my body onto my knees, letting him breathe properly.

'Gently, Brooke, gently,' he gasped, which I did, and felt that this nut of his was quite soft and so only sucked on it and moved it about with my tongue, feeling quite pleased with myself in doing this for the first time. 'It's getting late, Brooke,' he said next and so I let his testicle drop free as I moved and gave the eye of his cock a last kiss before getting up off of him.

We both were silent as we got dressed, his cock now looking rather limp as I saw it disappear inside his trousers. When clothed, he took me in his arms and gave me a kiss.

'Thank you, Brooke, it was just perfect,' he said when he broke off from the kiss and I just smiled at him and went off to make us some coffee before mom and Auntie came home. I took our coffee into the living room and sat down beside him as I gave him his cup. I looked at the coffee table expecting to see some dollar bills there but there wasn't.

'No money, Uncle Stevie?' I asked.

'Nope,' he said, sipping at his coffee.

'Why not?' I asked indignantly, sitting up straight and looking him in the eye.

'Well, is was you that wanted it this time, so it should be you giving me some dollars,' he said with a smug smile. I couldn't now remember which of us had wanted it first. Did I?

'That's not fair!' I cried.

'Why? You wanted to be sucked as much as I did and you wanted me to fuck you too. So I did,' a smug look on his face.

'I'll tell mom,' I threatened.

'Go ahead. Yeah, tell her how you wanted to be fucked and suck on my cock and see what will happen then. She'll tell your dad and then you'll be in real trouble.' Which was true, I would be grounded for he hadn't worn a condom and dad didn't know that I was on the pill.

'You bastard! That's blackmail,' I cried.

'Is it? If I'm a bastard and a blackmailer, you are a whore for you took the money,' he said, that smug expression still on his face.

'Fuck you then. That's the last time that you'll have your cock inside me,' I shouted at him as I got up and stormed off to the kitchen but at least I had calmed down before mom and Auntie came back from the Mall.

Mom and I soon left and went home where we had dinner and I pleaded tiredness and went off to bed where, after I'd got undressed, cursing my uncle and went and got Peter out and pushed it up into my pussy and switched it on and lay on my back and kept rubbing my tits as the vibrator teased my clit and throbbed inside me to give me my fourth orgasm of the day. As I sucked off my juices from this rubber cock, I thought that my best friend at school, Carli, might like to try this toy.

We had been friends even before we went to school, her living only a few doors away from our house, and so the next day, I got her to come round to my house after school and up to my bedroom. I know that she played with herself the same as I had before I'd got Peter for we didn't have any secrets from each other, and quite often spoke of how and what we did to our own pussy. But I was now drawing a line for now by not telling her that I had my uncle fuck me but told her that I'd now had several orgasms that had sent me higher than the moon.

With her wanting to know more about this was why she was now in my bedroom with me. She gave out a gasp when I showed her Peter and began to fondle it when I put it in her hand.

'Wow! Is this what a man's cock looks like?' she asked in awe, her eyes wide.

'Yes,' I said and leaned into her and twisted the base and started it off.

'Ooooh,' she cried as it began to vibrate in her hand. 'It feels funny,' her eyes still wide open as she then held it in both hands. 'And you put this inside you?'

'Yes. It's supposed to be the nearest you can get to feel what it would be like having a man doing it with his thing,' holding back that in reality it didn't hold a candle to the real thing. 'I thought you might like to try it.'

'Oooh, yes please,' she said, lifting her dress up and pulling down her panties.

'Lie back and let me put it in,' I said, taking it from her and sitting down next to her, looking down at her pussy that I could now see between her open legs. This wasn't the first one I'd looked at for I've seen most of the girls of our class when we've been in the showers after our sports, all needing to wash off the sweat from our bodies. It's strange how many of them washed themselves quickly and seemed to be shy in the others seeing their naked body. It didn't faze me and I'm sure that they all had seen all that I had, well to tell the truth, I really flaunted my naked body while there for I had at the time, the biggest tits and was quite proud of them.

Now with me having used a cucumber, I knew that it was that which broke through my hymen and guessed that Carli still had hers intact so I was going to put Peter inside her and break through for she might not want to when it reached her hymen. I pushed her dress up a bit more so that her stomach was bare and put my hand on it as I put Peter to the lips of her sex and worked just the head in between them.

'With it being your first time, Carli, you'll feel a little sharp pain at first but you'll then enjoy it,' I said as I began to push Peter into her and when I felt the thin barrier there, gave a quick push to break through and pushed it more until it could go no further.

'Oooh, ow,' she panted, looking up at me. 'I felt that pain as you said, but it's gone now and it feels funny inside me.'

'Wait for this then,' I said as I twisted the knob and started the vibrator and at the same time, ran my hand gently across her stomach at the same time.

'Oooh, aaah, wow!' she exclaimed as her legs closed, bringing her thighs together. 'This is fucking fantastic! I can really feel it and….oooh, oh my God!'

I knew then that the little knob on the end was exciting her clit now and had her lower body squirming about on the bed as she began to really get excited at having Peter pulsate away inside her. There were more groans of delight she gave, her eyes closed tight, screwing her face up a little. Then she started to buck under my hand and knew that she was about to orgasm. Her back arched and I could see the muscles of her thighs tighten as she gave out an enormous shudder that lasted several seconds before she relaxed and flopped back down on the bed.

'Jesus fucking Christ!' she cried, her eyes now open wide. 'Was that an orgasm?'

'Yes,' I laughed. 'Your first one eh?'

She gave out a giggle. 'Yes, and it was fucking great!'

'Well let me know what you think of this then,' I said as I moved further down the bed and got her legs open and pulled out Peter and put it in her hand. It was all shiny with her outcoming juices and could see that there was more coming out from her pussy. I quickly got in between her legs and used my shoulders to keep her thighs apart so that I could use my fingers to open her right up and dived in with my mouth and tongue and ate her pussy.

I could hear her groans as my tongue moved in and out of her vagina, giving the clit a few sweeps too that made her body give out a shiver. Her thighs came tight to my shoulders when she started to buck her hips a little, also forcing her body down closer to my mouth that was sucking at the juices that were still seeping out of her. I can't be that bad at cunnilingus for I brought her up to having her second orgasm though maybe it just might be the thrill of having me eat out her pussy for the first time. I lapped up the juices that seeped out of her body and quite liked the taste as I sucked and licked at her.

I looked up at her and was surprised to see her sucking on Peter, her eyes twinkling back at me as she tried to grin with her mouth full. I then moved up her thin body, kissing my way up from her stomach, wiping my mouth on it as I did so. I pushed her dress further up and onto one of her small, but growing tits to take a nipple into my mouth and gently teased it with my teeth as I sucked at the same time. She must have taken Peter out of her mouth as I heard her give out a groan and had a hand come down to my head and begin running her fingers through my hair. I did the same to the other tit before moving further up to lay on top of her to give her a kiss which she accepted and kissed me back with real passion. I think we both got a thrill out of the sucking of each other's tongue and I now had a raging heat in my belly and wanted her to do the same to me, leaving out the use of Peter.

'Will you now eat my pussy, Carli?' I asked as we broke off the kissing. I could feel her heart beating quite fast inside her chest with mine still pressed against it. 'Give me the same thrill and an orgasm?'

'Yes, Brooke,' she panted, 'and then you can do it to me again for it was fucking awesome.' I helped her get her dress right off and we rolled over to now have her on top of me as she kissed me on the lips before starting that trek down my body, kissing and sucking on my nipples until I gave her head a gentle push for her to carry on moving down. I opened my legs for her to slide her body in between them and gave out a shiver as I felt her fingers part the lips down there and have her hot breath waft over my exposed flesh.

I trembled at the first tentative touch of her tongue as it moved up and around my clit which made me give out a shudder and groan when her tongue touched it for the first time. I think this made her bolder for her tongue really began to rasp my clit and flit back and forth into the entrance to my vagina. It wasn't long before I had her push in as much as she could and have it flicking away inside me.

I could hear the lapping noise as she began taking in some of my juices that were now seeping out of me and I nearly giggled at wondering what she would think when she had my orgasmic fluid hit her mouth, which wasn't far off in the coming. I pressed and squeezed my tits as I got closer and closer and finally had the fire in my belly erupt like a volcano and gave her the lava that was my orgasm's fluid. I heard her cough, or was she choking at this outpouring as I thrashed about in the euphoric feeling that ran through my body at having this orgasm. The shudder and shaking of my body eased off as my body went limp as wave after wave of pleasure ran through me as Carli kept up her sucking of my pussy.

She licked me dry before moving up my body in the same way as I had done to her until she was right up on top of me and gave me kisses like she'd never done before.

'That was just great, Brooke,' she panted. 'Did I do it right?'

'Carli,' I panted, coming down from up high. 'I've not had better. You were terrific,' pulling her head down for another kiss.

'Will you eat me again?' she asked, breaking off the kisses. 'Make me cum again?'

'Of course, darling,' I said, and so we rolled over for the second time and I went down to eat her pussy and gave her another orgasm which made her a friend for life.

It was this first time of us having sex together that confirmed what I had thought that I was really a lesbian and had just now turned Carli into one too, for she wanted to eat my pussy as much as I wanted to eat hers, though actually turning her into a lesbian was with some doubt as she hadn't as yet, to my knowledge, had a man fuck her. Even today I'm not sure if she has or not. But back to then, that after this first session as it were, we began eating pussy at least once a week, if not twice, sometimes in my bedroom or in hers. She wasn't the only one that I converted to lesbianism as I grew older. The time came when I found out about my Auntie Mischelle, she was more than just being a friend of mom's.

It was mom and dad's eighth wedding anniversary and dad took her to Florida for a week's holiday as well as celebrating this event. At first mom objected to taking the week off away from the shop but as Auntie Mischelle had already spent some time helping mom in the shop, said that she would look after it for her as well as me so that she could have this vacation. As mom really did need a vacation, I piped up that I would help Auntie as it was the summer break, and so that was it. Off went mom and dad and I would go with Auntie to the shop.

Even though it was summer time now, we had lots of people come to the shop to buy the summer clothes for their own vacations, so I was getting to wear quite a few different dresses to show them off to the clients. They would point out one that they liked and I would go with Auntie into the back store room where I would strip off and had her help me put on the dress or frock that I was to parade in.

It was on our first day there when Auntie, with her being behind me as she tried to get one dress on me and had a bit of trouble getting it over my expanding tits. She rubbed her hands over both of them as she tried to pull the top down. I immediately got a thrill run through me at feeling her hands move over them and even put my own hands up over hers and gave them a squeeze.

'These are getting rather big, Brooke,' she said, 'and you should be wearing a bra now.' What really turned me on was that she didn't pull her hands out from under mine and I was getting that wonderful feeling in my tummy. 'You don't mind me touching them, do you, Brooke?'

'No, Auntie. I like them being touched and rubbed,' I said, my nipples having risen up to tight little nodules. 'I do it a lot myself.'

I wish I could have seen what kind of expression she had on her face as she slowly pulled her hands down from under mine, really feeling that my nipples had risen up at her touching them. She pulled the dress down and smoothed out the front so that I could go out and parade myself to the would be buyer. The woman was pleased with it and said that she would buy it, so back we went and had Auntie take it off of me, feeling my tits again as she did so.

That was our last sale of the day and the shop was soon closed and the other staff woman said her goodbyes and left the two of us alone.

'So you liked me rubbing your breasts, Brooke?' Auntie asked in a quiet voice as we moved towards the back of the shop where the office was.

'Yes, Auntie. It gave me a lovely thrill. Better than when I do it myself,' I replied. I was quite outspoken.

'Would you like me to do it again?' was the question, and knew then that she was into females as I knew I was then. 'You can also rub mine if you want to.' That was the clincher that she was a lesbian and wondered if she would go so far as to eat my pussy that was now feeling rather wet at her suggestions.

'I would like that,' I said and she took my hand and led me into the changing room where customers could try out dresses themselves. In there was a couch, well a sort of one for it was more like a large padded bench against one wall. Here, she sat down and pulled me towards her so that I was standing in front of her and let her lift up the dress I was wearing and pulled it up over my head to have me standing there in just my thin panties.

'They are a lovely pair,' she said, putting my dress to one side as she then put the palms of her hands on my breasts and began to rub them in a circular motion, making the nipples become upstanding again. 'Nice and firm and with lovely nipples that just beg to be kissed. Would you let me kiss them?'

'Yes, please,' I said, now squeezing my thighs together as I felt some of my pre-orgasmic fluid start to seep out of me. She pulled me in between her legs and held me close as she leaned her head forward and had her place her mouth over one teat and begin to suck on the nipple. She had her arms round my waist as she held me and I put my hands up onto her shoulders and so she felt me give out a little shudder as she began to really kiss, suck and then start to nibble at the upraised nipple.

'Oooh, that's nice,' I moaned as she got more adventurous with her hands, having them move up and down my back and sometimes giving the cheeks of my bum a squeeze with her fingers. I was in heaven at having another female nearly as old as my ma doing this to me, making me begin to squirm and having more of my juices wetting the gusset of my panties.

After several minutes of kissing both breasts, having gently squeezed the other one that she wasn't sucking upon, she eased me away from the couch for her to slip down onto her knees in front of me. Now in this position, her head moved further down over my rib cage, kissing every inch as well as licking me with her tongue. I was now shivering with delight as her tongue moved in and out of my belly button and nearly gasped when I felt her hand move up between my legs and feel the gusset of my panties.

'My, my. You're all wet down here,' she said as her fingers moved along the gusset, and saw her lift up those wet fingers and suck upon them. 'Would you like me to kiss you down there as well?'

'Ye…yes please. I think that would be nice too,' I said with a slight stammer, knowing damn well that it would be, wondering just what was she thinking in this seduction of me into having female sex. Little did she know at this point.

Her hands came up to my waist and pulled down my panties and I lifted each foot in turn so that she could take them right off. She then turned me round and gently eased me back to the couch for me to sit down where she then lifted my legs up onto it as she swiveled me round to be lying full length on it. She then moved round to the end and spread my legs apart as she laid her front down on the end of this couch and I gave out a shiver as her hands slowly moved up on the insides of my legs. Her fingers slowly kneading my inner thighs as they crept up ever closer to my pussy as she leaned in and I felt her hot breath stir the small hairs that were round my pussy and the fingers touched me there.

She must have felt me trembling as her fingers parted my sex lips and I felt her tongue slowly move in between them and sweep round the inside making more of my juices flow down and had her tongue take some into her mouth. My body jerked at the first touch of her tongue on my clit and couldn't help but give out a groan as a bolt of pleasure shot up deep into my belly.

It was as though a battery was being passed across my clit, giving me little electric shocks each time making my body spasm and building up the fire in my belly as well as having her tongue dive deep into the entrance of my vagina. I was dribbling out some of my juices and could hear the odd slurping noise as she sucked it into her mouth. It wasn't long before my head seemed to whirl around and I could see the many colors of the rainbow flashing through my eyes as I lifted up my hips to try and grind my pussy up to that questing tongue as I had my orgasm. Boy, it was a veritable flood with not having one so violent in its outpouring of my juices before.

I sagged back down onto the couch as Auntie still kept sucking and licking my pussy and my hands went down to stroke and run my fingers through her hair. That was the best one so far and I still had a lot to learn in eating pussy. She must have licked me dry before lifting her head up and began to kiss first my pussy hair and slowly crept up my body, kissing and licking across my stomach until she was half on top of my body and began kissing and nipping at my nipples in turn as well as sucking on them. I couldn't help groaning as she began to arouse me again and pulled her head up and kissed her, our mouths opening and our tongues began playing with each other and felt more of my juices coming out of me to run down between my thighs and in to the crack of my ass.

'Well? Did you like it?' she asked me after breaking off our kisses.

'Oh yes, Auntie,' I breathed and I'm sure my eyes were shining as hers were.

'Would…would you like to do the same to me?' she asked, and I could see the desire in her eyes and I really wanted to see, stroke and kiss those breasts that were pressing themselves to my small ones and really wet myself at the very thought of giving my aunt the same pleasure that she had given me.

'Er…well, er, yes if you'll let me,' I stammered, feeling my face blush. 'I'll do my best.'

Auntie Mischelle moved up off of me so that I could sit up as she began to take off her clothes. The top first to reveal her big breasts as her bra came off at the same time, large and full with lovely bright nipples in the center that just the sight of made my belly go all funny. My juices started to flow when she slipped down her skirt and panties to reveal the hairs of her pussy.

She smiled at me as she stepped out of them and laid herself down on her back on the couch, me moving out of the way for her to do this. I gave her a smile back, dragging my eyes away from her full breasts that still looked firm with her lying on her back. I moved in close and put my hand on the left tit and felt that is was firm and yet still soft to the touch. I then put my other hand on the right one and found it was the same as I began to rub my hands over them both, feeling the nipples start to harden as I did so.

'Press harder,' Auntie said as she closed her eyes as I began to push down a bit more as I rubbed them across the nipples. 'Now suck on them.'

I took my hand off the closest tit and leaned over and took the nipple in between my lips and began to suck on it as I kept giving it a squeeze as I did so. I brought my thighs together to try and stop my juices from running down my inner thighs without much success as I was thoroughly enjoying this sucking of a fully grown tit. Auntie was giving out little groans as I nibbled at her nipple and then moved my other hand down over her stomach and into the pubic hairs just above her pussy. Feeling where my hand was going, her legs opened and I was able to have my fingers move down to get them in between the soft lips of her sex.

I could feel her body squirm a little as I was then lying on her side as I began fingering her, feeling the softness of her insides except for the hard little nut of her clit. This I homed in on and began using my thumb to rub it as two of my fingers pushed themselves into the vaginal opening. She was wet already as they slipped in easily to be able to then move about, feeling the heat from the walls of her passage as well as the juices that were slowly oozing down round my fingers.

She gave out another groan and so I let her nipple slip out of my mouth and began to lick her as I moved my head further down her body as I eased my own up and slowly moved off of her to be able to get between her legs without stopping my kissing and licking of her as I moved. Down through her bush my tongue travelled until I was able to use my tongue on her clit and really give it a good licking as well as sucking on it. I felt her body quiver at the touch and increased the pressure of my tongue to raise it up even harder so that I was able to get my lips over it to squeeze it more and make her shake.

I could hear more groans as she felt two of my fingers slip into her now wet pussy and had the muscles inside her vagina begin to flex themselves around my fingers as they moved about inside her. More of her juices began to flow down and I then kept switching back and forth from clit to vagina to suck and take what I could into my mouth. Her body movements were becoming more erratic and her thighs kept squeezing themselves to the sides of my head as I kept on sucking and nibbling at her clit.

'I'm cumming! I'm cumming!' were her cries that I heard and felt her body tense and her hips began thrusting up to my mouth and her whole body seemed to lift up from the couch as she went rigid and had a copious amount of her fluid pour out of her vagina as she had her orgasm. It was like being under a faucet without a tap, there was that much of her orgasmic juices that came pouring out of her pussy. I nearly choked on it but kept on sucking and swallowing as well as licking her clit.

'Enough! Enough, Brooke,' she cried out, pulling my head up from between her thighs and pulling me to lie on top of her, our breasts getting squashed between us. She held the sides of my face as she kissed me, smearing her juices over both our lips, well mine were already covered in her cum.

'You've done this before, Brooke,' she panted after breaking off our kissing. 'You suck pussy just like your mom.'

'What?' I reared up, her face going red at the gaffe she'd just made. 'My mom? You and her have…have…,' I ran out of words as I saw the look in her eyes. Her arms came round my back and pulled me down as she gave me another kiss.

'Yes, we have. Your mom and I have been lovers for years now,' she said softly.

'But…but…what…does dad know?' I stuttered.

'Yes. He's even been in bed with us,' she said with a dreamy smile on her face. I was lost for words. Mom and Auntie? Lovers? And dad knowing all about it. It didn't make sense. It was another year before I made sense of it when I found out that he had had a lover too. Her name was Bernadette, but we'll come to that later.

So here I was, having sex with my Auntie, well her not really being my aunt, but my mom's lover with her now having had both of us. But that didn't stop us now from having sex every day after the shop had closed while mom and dad were on holiday.

Now before they had actually gone for that holiday, the question was raised about me being left at home all alone, I hadn't then understood why mom didn't want me sleeping over at Auntie's place and accepted my suggestion that I slept over at Carli's house. Now what we had cooked up together was that we told her mother that Carli had been invited to sleep over at my place for the week and we got her to agree to this. So every night I had Carli in bed with me, where we had sex before sleeping and in the afternoon at the shop I would have sex with Auntie Mischelle.

With Carli's mom and dad not knowing that mine were away for the week, gave her a spare door key so that she could get into my house and she was there when I got home from the shop. I was greeted with a kiss from her when I entered and before you could say Washington, we were in my bedroom with our clothes off and on my bed. We lay on our sides as we kissed, rubbing not only our breasts between us but had our legs entwined so that our pubes could move against each other. She was hornier than me and couldn't wait to push me onto my back and had her start to kiss first one breast, sucking on the nipple before giving it a little chew with her teeth making it rise up to a hard bud. Then it was over to the other tit to do the same as she rubbed the one already kissed and raised up hard.

I opened my legs for her to slither down in between as she kissed her way down, pausing for a little while to suck on each nipple, giving both a gentle nibble, making them stand up like little cones on a mountain top. Though my tits were not yet what you would call mountains like they are now. Many a girl wished that she had breasts like mine and even had one young gay male say the same thing. He had the face of a girl with a lovely head of hair but it would have looked incongruous to have tits like mine and a prick between his thighs. I didn't really know about transvestites then but I do now. That it wasn't only men who dressed up and acted as a woman, but some women would also dress up as men and were known as being butch.

But Carli was now down between my legs and felt her fingers open the lips of my sex and her hot breath waft around the insides as her tongue flicked in to catch a drop of my juices that had already started to flow. Now came the pleasant jolts as her tongue next hit my clit in swift strokes to make my body shiver in delight as her fingers now entered the entrance to my now wet cavern.

I had a job to stop my hands from clenching as my body gave out shivers at what she was doing and could only stop them from doing this by bringing them up to my tits and squeezing them hard as I felt my orgasm building up under the ministrations of Carli's fingers and tongue. It's an agonizing thrill you feel as you approach your orgasm and your body is shaking and you cannot stop that little scream as your whole body becomes a fire and then to have that internal body explosion as you have that blissful orgasm that erupts and floods your inner self with not only your fluids but the relief that spreads throughout and you become like jelly.

I lay there like a deflating rubber doll as Carli drank my juices with a slurping noise until she had taken it all and still continued to lick me until it was all gone before she pulled herself up my body, kissing every part till our lips met in a passionate kiss. This went on for several minutes, our tongues talking to each other as they played around in our mouths before we broke apart, both breathing heavily.

'My turn now,' Carli breathed out, her eyes bright and shiny. So I slowly moved down her body after one more kiss on the lips before kissing her neck and then one nipple of her heaving breasts. She gave out a groan and felt her body squirm slightly as she felt my teeth gently pinch that nipple between them. I sucked on that tit for a few minutes before attending to the other one, making her give out another groan. My tongue ran all the way down her lower chest and gave her belly button a poke before moving into the slight pubic hairs that she had there.

Her legs opened wider for me to settle in between them, using my shoulders to keep her thighs apart as I began using my tongue to open up the lips of her sex to dive in and start to give her the same thrill that she had given me. I felt her legs twitch as my tongue touched her clit for the first time as it moved over the small bud and with me doing this several times, it came up to be as hard as a nut. I didn't take long to have her squirming under my ministrations of her sex. Her thighs trying to close which I had prevented with my shoulders being there as she began to moan and I could feel that her hands were pounding the bed until she went rigid.

Her scream could have woken the dead it was so loud as she had her orgasm, flooding my mouth and covering my chin with the outpouring of her juices until I felt her body slump back down on the bed as I continued to take as much as I could of her succulent juice. Her thighs had relaxed with having had her release and I was then able to move and I slithered up her sweaty body to mash our tits together as she pulled me tight to her chest to kiss me with a passion that she had never done before.

'Brooke, Brooke, Brooke,' was all she could gasp out between kisses and gulps of air as she panted away. Her eyes shining like bright stars from the skies as she held me tight to her body for me to feel her thumping heart which was now beginning to slow down as she came down from that highest of peaks that a female could reach with having sex as we had just done between us.

'I love you, Brooke,' she said, now, with her coming down to earth, was able to speak properly, kissing me again and getting her own fluid smeared over her lips and chin from my face.

'I love you too, Carli,' I panted, trying to get breath into my body with her squeezing my so tightly to her wet body.

'Can we do this again?' she asked as she still hugged me.

'Every night for a week,' I said and had her squeeze me again before I was able to prise myself out from her embrace.

We had more sex between us that first night, both of us having our orgasms and as I had said, for the rest of the week too. It was a delightful breakfast that we had together before she went off home while I went to the shop where I was greeted by Auntie Mischelle with a kiss. I modeled two dresses that day that were then sold and overall, it was a good day for sales which pleased Auntie and when the last of the staff left at the end of the day, I was kissed again and taken into the changing room where we both took our clothes off and had sex again between us.

This we did for the whole week where when the shop closed, we would have sex together, Auntie going down on me first after kissing and nibbling at my tits and nipples. Then going between my legs to tease me with her tongue roving over my clit as well as diving in and out of my vagina, bringing me up to that heavenly delight of having an orgasm.

Then I would do the same to her, learning a lot as to how to really chew pussy and bring about an early orgasm which pleased Carli no end. It was a grand week having Auntie during the day and Carli at night, having countless orgasms with the week passing by in a flash so it seemed before Mom and Dad came back from their holiday.

Carli had gone to her home and I was with Auntie Mischelle in our house when they arrived. I got a kiss from Mom and Dad and Auntie got a big kiss and a hug from Mom. Dad disappeared into his office room as Mom and Auntie prepared a meal as they talked while I saw to laying the table for dinner. Auntie didn't stay and so it was just the three of us to sit down for our meal.

Hardly a word was spoken as we ate and I'm sure that I could feel a certain tension in the air with the silence and didn't know what it was until later the next day. It was still silence as I helped Mom do the dishes after dinner and I was soon packed off to bed, wondering what was going on.

I was even more bewildered next morning, when Mom gave me a big hug and a kiss. 'Auntie Mischelle is taking you to the shop today. Be a good girl. I love you,' she said giving me another hug and kiss before ushering me out of the house where Auntie was waiting to go with me to the shop.

The day went by okay and I was surprised that we didn't have sex when the shop closed and was walked home by Auntie who gave me a kiss at my door telling me to be a good girl before going off to her own home. I went indoors to find the house empty but didn't give much thought to not seeing Mom there preparing dinner. So I started to get things ready as a surprise for her and it was an hour before Dad came home.

'Mom's not home yet,' I said to him in a greeting and got a surprise myself as he hugged me and gave me a kiss on the cheek before going off to have a wash without saying a word. I started doing the dinner and the pot roast was simmering in the oven when Dad came into the kitchen. 'Well dinner's in the oven and we'll have it when Mom gets home.' He had gone and sat down at the table and beckoned me over and took me into his arms and hugged me.

'She's not coming home,' he said in a thick sounding voice that I'd never heard before. 'She's left me. Left us.'

Fuck! What a bombshell to drop on me and I now felt him quivering in his embrace as his words sank into my mind. Mom? Mom gone and left us? Tears came to my eyes as I remembered that kiss last night and the words that she loved me. I was sobbing as I got the pot roast out of the oven and dished it out onto two plates and not three and put them on the table and sat down. But I couldn't eat and halfway through dad eating his, broke down in tears having hardly touched mine and left the table and ran up to my room. I was still crying in bed when dad came in later and sat on the edge of my bed and stroked my hair but not saying anything and after a few minutes got up and left.

Breakfast was a somber meal, neither of us two speaking as we ate until he gave out a big sigh and got up and left the kitchen. I heard knocking at the front door and went and opened it to find Auntie Mischelle standing there.

'Well, are you coming to the shop with me,' and I knew by her tone of voice that she knew that Mom had left us. I dumbly nodded and got my coat and went off to the shop with her. She held my hand the whole way, giving it a squeeze now and then. It was during a lull in the shop that we finally spoke.

'When did you know that Mom was leaving us?' I asked, fighting to hold back my tears.

'Last night. That's when she told me and asked me to not only look after the shop but you too. Well,' she began in a shaky voice, 'we have been looking after each other for the past week.' I couldn't help but give her a shy smile at this reference to us having had sex over that time.

'Will…will we still look after each other tonight, when the shop shuts?' I asked, looking down at my feet not being able to really face her with this question.

'Of course we will, Brooke,' she said, taking me into her arms and giving me a hug. 'I love you as I loved your mother.'

Wow! Did she love mom as she did me? Sex wise, was the thought that ran through my mind.

'Did...did you and...and mom do what we do?' I asked, my voice trembling, wanting and yet not to really know the truth.

'Yes, Brooke,' she said, giving the top of my head a kiss. 'And I will look after you as she asked me to.'

'Did...did she know that we made love to each other?' my voice muffled because I had my face buried between her breasts.

'I think she might have guessed but I didn't tell her. You can always stay over at my house some nights for I need company too,' she said.

'What about Uncle Stevie?' I asked, now leaning back and looking up at her.

'Oh, he's not there now. He's left.'

'What! With Mom?' I cried.

'No,' she said with a little laugh. 'He left a month or so ago. Besides, your mom wouldn't have gone with him at all. No siree. They never really got on with each other and he would have been the last person she would have left your dad for. Now buck up and think of what we can do later.' She smiled down at me and pressed her breasts towards my face and knew that was what I wanted.

There in the shop that day, I got to model two dresses for customers, not minding in the least being watched as I took my own dress off to be naked in front of the customer, her husband and Mischelle. She had told me to drop calling her auntie as she wasn't really my aunt but to call her by name.

I could see the lascivious look in the man's eyes as they roved over my naked body for I wasn't wearing any panties and I got a thrill at letting him see me like this. It's when his eyes dropped from looking at my breasts down to my labia, that I felt myself starting to get wet there. So when I took this dress off for the woman to buy, her back now towards me, I let the man see me run my fingers up between the lips and then put them into my mouth to suck off the juices that had started to flow there. His face had turned a little shade of red and he gave his lips a lick with his tongue and guessed that he would have liked to have had his tongue where my fingers had been.

That was in the morning and it didn't surprise me when he came back into the shop in the afternoon without his wife and asked Mischelle that he would like to buy another dress for his daughter. I smiled to myself as he sat there and watched me take my own dress off to show him my naked body again before I put the one he wanted to look at on. But that really wasn't the dress he wanted and I had to model four for him, though I really began to tease him by first rubbing my breasts and then running my finger through my slit and then sucking on it. I even dropped a dress as I turned away from and bent down so that he could see my bare ass, taking my time in picking it up.

Twice I saw him have to move on the chair he was sitting on, seeing that he had an erection inside his trousers and was trying to make it more comfortable in there. I gave him a sweet smile to let him know that I knew what he was doing and why he had come back. I really teased him in the dressing and undressing the four dresses before he finally decided on the last one. Mischelle had noticed what I was doing and guessed why.

'Brooke,' she began after he had left the shop. 'I think you are turning into a slut the way you acted with that man.'

'He bought a dress, didn't he?' I countered. 'He got what he came for,' and couldn't help giving out a snigger. 'He would have liked to do what we will do soon. We will, won't we, for I'm getting right horny just thinking of it?'

'So am I, so let's close down now,' she said and went and told the other girl that the shop was now closing and sent her off home and locked the front door and came back to me and I followed her into the changing room where we both began to take our clothes off. It was nice to see her big tits move the way they did when she took her bra off and couldn't wait any longer and quickly moved in and took a nipple into my mouth to suck on.

'Wait, you slut,' she said, pulling her nipple back out of my mouth. 'Let's do it in comfort,' and carried on till she was naked the same as I was now.

'See to me first, Mischelle, I'm soaking wet already,' I said as I lay down on my back on the couch and opened my legs for her to see just how wet I was down there. She didn't need asking a second time for she was soon on her knees and had her fingers opening me right up to dive in with her tongue. Oh what bliss it was to feel her tongue rove over my clit, every touch of it sent sparks of electricity run up through my body. Then back into the entrance of my vagina, making more juices flow which she was licking up like a bitch on heat. But then I was a bitch too for I was on heat and it was building up inside me as I rose higher and higher before bursting out like a thunderstorm.

Lightning flashed through my closed eyes as my body shivered and shook for it was like a clap of thunder as I had my orgasm. Flooding Mischelle's mouth with my cumming as I came down from the heaven that she had sent me with just the use of her tongue.

I mauled my tits with my hands as I squeezed them in the thrill I had just had, the nipples up as hard as nuggets that I then nipped with my fingers before rubbing them as I slowly began to relax and sink back into the cushioning couch. My legs were now wide open and I could hear the slurping noise she made as she kept on sucking on my pussy.

'That was fucking lovely,' I gasped, managing to now be able to breathe having got fresh oxygen into my lungs. 'Much better than Carli.'

'Who's Carli?' Mischelle asked, her head having come from between my thighs, her mouth and chin all wet and shiny with my juices.

'My school girl friend,' I panted, still really out of breath. 'She's been sleeping with me over the past week while…while mom and dad were away,' the pain coming back to me that my mom had really left me. Left me with dad and now not having her give me a cuddle before I went to bed.

'Well now it's your turn to show me what you do to her,' she said as she leaned up and over my stomach which she kissed, smearing it with my juices from her chin and lips. It was an effort for me to straighten up, feeling so exhausted after having that tremendous orgasm under Mischelle's administration between my legs. She moved away for me to roll off the couch and for her to stretch her body out and opened her arms for me to climb on top of her to be embraced and us to kiss each other.

I could feel that the nipples of her tits were up and hard as they got squashed by mine in the long kiss we had, our tits as well as our stomachs against each other and my legs between hers for her trimmed mound to grind against mine that didn't have half the pubic hair that she had. I eased myself down her naked body until I could take a nipple of her tit into my mouth to suck and gently nibble on it, raising it even harder than it was from the rubbing of our tits together. I spent a minute or two on seeing to this one before moving my head over to do the same to the other one.

Not showing any preference to either tit, gave it the same amount of time in the sucking of it before moving down a little more to be able to run my tongue underneath the full breast, tasting the slight saltiness of her perspiration that had collected there. Moving down and kissing her rib cage until I was doing the same to her stomach, using my tongue to delve into the indentation of her navel.

Her legs had already opened for my body to slide down between them as I buried my nose into her pubic hairs, getting her odor as my tongue parted them to push down to the lips of her labia. Now I brought my fingers into play to open them for my tongue to move in between them and run it all round, evading her clit at this time to make her body twitch with me giving a darting poke of my tongue into her vagina.

Having started her on the road to her orgasm, it was now time to tackle her clit with my tongue as my fingers began to move inside her. The inside muscles began to play with my moving fingers as I brought her clit up enough to be able to use my teeth to gently nip it in between sucking on it. These were intermittent as I needed to breathe occasionally for having my nose pressed into her pubes, but kept arousing her at the same time until I felt her thighs began to become taut and squeeze in towards me as she approached the build up and then had her whole body begin to convulse as she began having her orgasm.

It was a veritable flood that began to fill my mouth and I nearly choked as it flowed out, quite a lot running down my chin as I swallowed what I had there, quickly so as to get more and please her with doing so. My tongue now moving inside her vagina, lapping away until the flood subsided and felt her begin to relax, hearing a big sigh that she gave and the pummeling of the couch stop that she had been beating with her fists.

I now moved back up her body, smearing her stomach with her own juices from my chin as I did so until I was fully up on top of her and into her open arms for a passionate kiss.

'Brooke, oh Brooke! That was the best yet,' she panted as the kiss broke off. 'You definitely have been learning some.' Her eyes were sparkling and her hugging of me was strong and I could feel her heart still pounding away, it being transmitted as throbs through her breasts that were being squashed against mine. I slowly lifted my body up from hers, hearing and feeling that sucking sound as we came apart and got off the couch. 'Pity we haven't got a shower here,' she said as she sat up and picked her clothes up from the floor as I did and we both got dressed. She gave me a hug when we were ready to leave the shop and we went off home, her to hers and me to mine, sad that mom wouldn't be there.

Dad wasn't either but I knew he would be home soon, so I started doing dinner and it was ready when he arrived, looking as miserable as I felt. It was a quiet meal and I was glad when he went into his office and left me to watch the television, but that didn't help my mood and so soon went to bed to cry.

But time passed with me going to help Mischelle in the shop and having sex afterwards and it wasn't long before it was back to school. Carli would often come home with me when school day finished and we would have sex together because she liked playing with Peter. Having it stuck up inside her pussy as she was between my legs eating me out. That was because I couldn't take Peter to her house. Saturdays I helped Mischelle in the shop where after closing we would have fun together on the couch and it was on some Sundays that I would go round to her house where we could fuck each other in her bed.

Both of my birthdays came and went and it was close to another birthday when Bernadette really came into my life. I had known her for several years now what with her being a dental assistant and seeing her once a year for my check on my teeth. Now somebody must have spoken out of turn in the fact that I liked having oral sex with another female, because she now, out of the dentist's hearing remarked that I had a lovely pair of breasts now that I was older and that she admired them.

I had sat myself in the dentist chair and she put a bib on me up under my chin and used her hand to straighten out the front when she said this to me, her hand moving more than once down the front of the bib, feeling them beneath it.

'They must be as big as mine,' she said, running her hands down the front of her tunic emphasizing them. 'Your dad and I used to be friends you know,' which was something that I didn't. 'I'd like to be your friend too. Would you like to have dinner with me one night?' I didn't quite know what to say to this and it wasn't until I saw her lick her lips with the tip of her tongue did I get an inkling that she was intimating that it might be more than dinner. An old friend of dad? There was more in that and maybe I would find out.

'Yes, I'd love to,' I said before the dentist then came to the chair to check out my teeth, pleased that they were looking fine he said. After rinsing my mouth out, Bernadette wiped my chin and lips with a tissue, giving me a smile. 'I finish here at five. Will you meet my outside?'

'Yes,' I replied. 'I'd better go home and leave dad a note.'

'No need for that. I'll give him a ring and let him know,' she said.

'Okay,' I said, knowing that I only had to wait half an hour and it wasn't till I was outside did a thought struck me. How did she know dad's work phone number? Food for thought as I went and spent what time I had left to wait for Bernadette, looking at the shops in the Mall.

I got back to the surgery just as she was coming out and we went off to her home which wasn't that far from where I lived and we were soon inside. 'Would you like a drink?' she asked as we went into the kitchen.

'A Cola if you got one,' I replied.

'One Cola coming up,' she said as she opened the fridge and passed me a can as she got a beer out for herself. We both popped our cans and took a sip as she then began to get out things for our dinner. I sat and watched as she did this, offering to help but was told to stay sitting down as I was the guest. It was after a wonderful meal where I insisted on doing the washing up before we went into the sitting room where she started to make her play for me.

'As I said in the surgery, Brooke, you got a lovely pair of breasts,' her hand stroking my arm. 'And lovely skin too,' and I gave her a smile. 'Lovely teeth too as you know. You should smile more often as they are one of your best features, apart from your breasts that is,' giving me a smile back. 'Your lips too look as though they would be nice to kiss. So much that I would like to kiss them. Would you let me?' her eyes shining as she moved her face closer towards me. I had tingles running up all over my body and butterflies in my stomach and an ache in my groin. I gave a nod and so she kissed me.

It was a soft one as were her lips on mine as she kissed which I liked and leaned in closer to her to really feel mine pressing against hers. They parted and felt her tongue push against my teeth and so opened my mouth and had her tongue move in and begin to play with mine. I didn't stop her hand from coming up and covering my breast for her to mould it in her hand as it moved over it, raising up my nipple. This I knew she felt for I wasn't wearing a bra and she gave out a little moan as she rubbed it while still playing with my tongue.

Her hand left my breast and took hold of my hand and brought it up to one of hers and pressed my hand up against it before returning to rub mine. I could feel that her nipple was up and hard and knew that she wasn't wearing a bra either, though I could swear she had been wearing one when in the surgery. She must have taken it off before she left, but I was now past caring for I wanted now to suck on what I could feel and she didn't stop my hand from moving to the inside of her blouse to take the full breast into the palm of my hand to continue rubbing the teat. This gave her license to do the same to me and was soon massaging mine.

'Brooke,' she began, breaking off the kissing. 'Will you take your top off so that I can kiss what I'm holding and you can kiss mine if you want to.'

Now we were getting down to it and so withdrew my hand from her tit and quickly opened my shirt and pulled it off with her taking her blouse off so that we both were then naked from the waist up. She smiled at me and eased me back on the sofa we were sitting on and played with one tit as she kissed and began to suck on the other. Her full breasts now pressing against my lower stomach as I gave myself up to the pleasure of her sucking and nibbling at my nipples making me become rather wet between my thighs.

She kissed, sucked, nibbled and licked all round my breasts for several minutes before lifting her head up off me and her body as she sat up.

'You taste and smell gorgeous, Brooke. Would you like to suck on mine now?' I looked down to really see that she had a beautiful pair that were just begging to have the same done to her. I think that the smile I was giving her was saying yes, so she stood up and held out her hand for me to take and stand up too. 'We'd be more comfortable if we used a bed,' she said smiling back at me and led me off to her bedroom. It was nice and quite airy and instead of getting straight on the bed, undid the belt of her skirt and let it drop to the floor and then took her panties off before getting on the bed. 'It's more comfortable without clothes getting in the way.'

What else could I do but strip off too and got onto the bed and straight into her open arms for her to kiss me. Her body was nice and smooth as was her kiss as she eased me down so that I could then suck and kiss her tits. I must say it was lovely to suck and kiss the breasts she had and considering that she was as old as my dad. Dad! I still hadn't asked her at how she knew his office phone number, must ask her later I thought as I kissed and sucked on her tits.

It wasn't long before she rolled me over to kiss me and then go down and start to eat my pussy. God, I was taken to heaven with the expertise she used in chewing me out with her teeth, tongue, mouth and fingers. It wasn't long before she brought about my orgasm and liberally flooded her mouth and face with the copious amount of fluid that I gave up to her wonderful administrations to my pussy.

Needless to say that after she had kissed me with her wet mouth, giving me a taste of my own juices, I went down on her and gave nearly as good a seeing to as she had to me. After which, we lay together as we kissed and stroked each other as well as some fingering of our pussies.

'How did you know dad's office phone number?' I finally got round to asking her.

'He gave it to me a long time ago,' she replied.

'How long was a long time ago?' I asked.

'We grew up and went to school together,' she said.

'How close were you?'

'Closer than we are now,' she said with a smile.

'The only closer you can get would be if he was inside you. Did you fuck?' I wanted to know.

'Yes. For a while, until we drifted apart with us both going to different colleges. Then he met your mum and they ended up getting married,' she said somewhat wistfully.

'So you've had sex with dad and now with me. Keeping it in the family so to speak,' I said in a wry voice. 'Well now that mom's gone, will you get together again?'

'No.'

'Why not?

'Well…no. I shouldn't tell you,' This pushed me into badgering her to tell me why she wouldn't until she eventually gave in and told me. 'He's gay.'

'What!' I exclaimed, sitting bolt upright, my tits bouncing up and down.

'Yes. He goes with other men sometimes. It was while he was at college that he began having sex with other boys there,' she told me. Wow! And there was I thinking that she and dad might get together again and maybe, with dad not really being my father, maybe we could have made it a threesome as it wouldn't really be incest with me having sex with him at the same time as Bernadette. I had already pictured the three of us in bed together, my mind had been moving faster than we had spoken. Him fucking me while I was sucking on Bernadette and then with it being the other way round not counting that I could suck on his cock as I had to

Stevie's while she sucked on my tits. This all dissolved with her saying no to them getting together again.

'Wow!' I said again, laying back down and feeling randy again at the images I still had in my mind and began to start having another session with Bernadette.

***

Having dinner and then sex with Bernadette became a monthly event for the pair of us from that evening onwards. I wondered if dad knew or guessed that was what we did every time I was round at her house. Though when I saw dad that evening after my first session with Bernadette, I saw him in a different light. Tried to picture him having sex with another man and looked back at the time he bought me the sex toys and watched me use them and wondered why he hadn't made any advances on me. But then guessed it was because of mum that he didn't, but with her now having left her, did he go with other men for sex? I had no answer to this at the time.

Time, being relative, seemed to fly by, and I began to badger and coerce dad into giving me driving lessons. He finally gave in and so on Sundays, he'd drive us to the old disused airfield and there, not being on a public road, began to show me how to drive, going up and down the old runway. Gear changing, reversing, parking and all the rest and got him to promise to buy me a car when I passed my driving test as I picked up the driving business quite fast.

My birthday came round and I had a great time. Dad took me, Carli, Bernadette and Mischelle to a posh restaurant where we had a lovely meal and even had a birthday cake brought in by one of the waiters with burning candles on top and everybody sang Happy Birthday to me. When I suggested that we all go to a disco place, dad cried off as he had to get up early for work but said that we all could go.

After dad left us after giving me a kiss and a hug, but Bernadette and Mischelle, being twice over the age of Carli and myself, said that they'd rather not go but wouldn't mind spending the rest of the evening at Mischelle's place for a few drinks. They must have spoken to each other about this, for that's where we went and it turned into a foursome of sex.

It was only after a few drinks that this was suggested. Carli being a little shy at first but she was soon as naked as us and didn't mind having Mischelle between her legs and eating her pussy while Bernadette was eating mine. Then it was turnabout and Carli was then down and seeing to Mischelle as I saw to Bernadette. We later, after a short rest, swapped partners and began all over again.

With me being the party girl, I got most of the attention and it was glorious at having both nipples sucked and nibbled on while having a tongue running over my clit as well as diving into my cave. I was in heaven! It was so great for all four of us that we exhausted ourselves and fell asleep with our bodies entwined all looking a right mess in the morning, covered in lipstick and sweat and sore nipples. We each had a shower, poor Mischelle, being last only had cold water as the boiler had run out of hot when it was her turn.

Two days later I had my driving test and passed! I was over the moon. I think the guy that took me spent more time looking at my tits than what I was doing, for I wore a loose low front blouse and no bra. So later, with my brand new driving license, went and saw Marica who worked at a car dealer that sold Honda's. She was a Latin American girl and had spoken to her several times when looking over the cars on the lot before getting my license, so we knew each other reasonably well.

'Hi, Brooke,' she greeted me. 'Did you pass your test?' Her knowing that I had applied and taken it. She already had hers, being four years older than me and had got this plum of a job in the sales department of this Honda dealer. She was rather blatant about her figure and quite often showed quite a bit of tit to prospective buyers and I'm sure that she let them have a good feel so that she could sell them a car. Like me, she never wore a bra and flaunted what she had.

'Yes,' I gushed, waving my driving license at her. 'Dad has said that he would buy me a car, so I would like to do a test drive on one of the cars.'

'No way! I'd lose my job if you trashed it,' she said.

'Aw, come on, Marica,' I pleaded. 'How am I going to know if the car I want is good enough. You'd be in the car with me to put me right if you thought I was doing something wrong. Come on! I'll do anything you want.' A foolish thing to say really.

'Well,' she said, saying it with a drawl, looking at not only my face but my breasts. She reached out her hand and finger one of my nipples. 'If you got your nipples pierced and had rings put in, I'd take a chance.' It was blackmail but I so wanted to do a test run. I looked at her ears which had been pierced to take her earrings and so had to ask the question.

'Did it hurt when you had your ears done?'

'Naw! Well, just a little but I'm glad I did,' she said, fingering one of the rings. 'It's quite easy and doesn't take long.' So after talking a little more, finally agreed to go with her during her break to a jeweler that did hers. Into the back of the shop we went after picking out two small gold rings where I had to take off my top and sit down. It didn't take long and she had lied for it did hurt, but once he had started, I had to let him do both of my nipples. He put the rings in and told me that I had to keep moving them around so that the flesh would heal properly and not have the rings become stuck so that I could later take them out if I wanted to.

So after paying for the piercing and the two rings, we went to a coffee shop for a quick bite to eat, which I had to pay for too, before we went back to the showroom and she picked out a car that I could test. She drove it first out of the yard until we were off the main streets and she then let me get behind the wheel. It was great! So exhilarating and exciting that I went and wet my panties. She told me to drive to the college campus, the college where I would soon be staying at. As we got there, Marica shocked me, but then I had got used to her quirks, for she pulled her top off and as

I drove past some of the students, she would flash her tits at them. I'm sure my face was quite red in embarrassment and it was difficult to concentrate on my driving.

I was also allowed to drive down the main road and into the parking lot of the dealer and knew that it was one of these cars that I wanted dad to buy for me. He did and I was over the moon when I drove it away from the plot with him as my first passenger in my new car. He said that he was impressed with my driving and was even given a beer when we got back home intact.

I had a few sex sessions with Marica later in between having the others and got me to take some pictures of her.

***

It was a week later when dad phoned me at home. He'd not long left for work and I had just washed up the breakfast things.

'Brooke. I've just had a guy on the phone who I sold a house to yesterday,' he began. 'He wants me to find him somebody to give the house a good clean and I thought that you might like to earn some money. Do you want to do it?'

'Great, dad. I could do with some extra for gas for the car,' I said. 'Where is the house?'

'Don't worry, I'll pick you up as I've got to go out to meet another client and I'll drop you off on the way and you can phone me to pick you up when you've finished,' he said. I told him okay and would be waiting for him. This he did about half an hour later and took me to this house that needed cleaning. I asked him about cleaning materials and he told me that the house had plenty there and he also told me that the guy's name was Brad Chevoski. Well he dropped me off and I waved him goodbye before going up to the house and ringing the bell.

'Hello?' said the man who answered the door. He was about six foot, age around his late thirties at a guess.

'Mr. Chevoski?' I asked and got a nod in reply. 'I'm Brooke and I've come to do a house clean,' I said.

'Great! I've been expecting you. Come in,' he said, standing aside for me to enter, which I did.

'I was told that you had all the cleaning materials that I would need, is that right?' I asked.

'Yes. This way. The cleaning cupboard is the narrow door under the stairs,' and showed me where it was. So with what I needed, I started work. The top floor first and did a good job of the three bedrooms and their bathrooms and got a call from him to say that he'd made some sandwiches and I noticed that it was one o'clock and so went downstairs and into the kitchen where he had them on the table there along with some beer.

We chatted while I ate and drank the beer before starting back to work and it was close on five when I felt that I had done enough and knew that I had done a good job. Back down in the lounge where he took me and poured me out a drink. I was that thirsty and so downed it almost in one gulp and he poured me another. Now I think that he must have spiked those drinks with something for I had never felt so relaxed before and laughed at the silly jokes he told me. He then took a handkerchief out of his pocket and wiped my forehead with it.

'You look as if you could do with a shower,' he said. 'Why don't you pop upstairs and get yourself cleaned up.' I now felt that I did need one and so I finished my third drink and went up to one of the bedrooms where I took my clothes off and went into the bathroom and turned on the spray and got under the streaming water.

I should have been shocked when I suddenly felt his naked body come up against mine, but I wasn't. This is why I think that my drinks had been spiked so I didn't react as I should have done. His body was up against mine and I could feel his erection being pressed up against the cheeks of my bum and didn't object when his hands came round my front to fondle my tits. After a few minutes of arousing me like this, he slowly turned me round and kissed me, pressing his erect cock up against my stomach.

His hands then came up onto my shoulders and began to push me down and I could do no more than let my leg muscles go and sink down onto my knees and had him push the head of his cock into my mouth. Above the sound of the water falling on top of me, heard him give out a sigh as he slowly moved it back and forth in my mouth as he now held my head still with his hands. What really annoys me now was the fact that I was loving it, having his cock move where it was as he face fucked me. But he didn't come and pulled himself out and lifted me up from my knees and turned off the water.

'Let's dry you off,' he said, getting me out of the shower and I just stood there as he rubbed my body dry with a towel before half drying himself. All I had eyes for then was his erect cock moving from side to side as he rubbed me down and then dried parts of himself before leading me out of the bathroom and pushed me onto the bed. He passed me another drink in a glass which I took and emptied it, giving it back to him to put on one side before getting onto the bed with me.

He kissed me first as he rubbed my tits before moving down the bed to lick and suck on them, my nipples as well with them being up and as hard as nuts. His hand wasn't idle as it came between my legs and I had his fingers move up inside me. The last man to do this was Stevie, but I just didn't seem to have the strength in me to stop him. Not even when he rolled on top of me and used his knees to part my legs. I lay there like a limp rag doll as I felt his cock move up into me and had to see the smile on his face as he then fucked me. Moving himself in and out of me until his body stiffened and had him come inside me, giving me his seed and mentally thanked the fact that I was now used to taking birth control pills on a daily basis.

When he'd finished with filling me with his sperm, he collapsed on top of me, squashing my breasts and I could feel his heart thumping away as he panted for more breath. I could feel his cock starting to shrink and slowly move out of me along with some of his sperm until it was right out and he rolled off of me.

There was a phone on the table by the side of the bed on his side that he picked up and dialed a number. I only caught a few words like, 'come round' and something like 'poontang' before he put the phone down. He lay there stroking my tits for about ten minutes before we heard the door bell ring. He got up and disappeared and was back a few minutes later with another man who looked at me lying there naked as he then took his clothes off and got onto the bed.

Before I knew it, he was on top of me and had his cock pushed up inside me as he began to fuck me. My head was then pulled to one side and had Brad's cock, which was now up hard again, pushed into my mouth. So I had to suck on him while his friend fucked me.

They both fucked me twice that night and made me suck on their cocks after they had pulled out of me before I finally passed out, now whether it was the drink or sheer tiredness, I don't know. I suddenly came awake and lifted my head then wished I hadn't for I had a blinding headache but was still able to see that it not yet morning for it was still dark outside. I felt really unclean being fully aware of what went on that night and saw that there was only the one man on the bed with me, the one whose house it was. The other must have left sometime after I'd fallen asleep. I saw by the bedside clock that it was just coming up to five in the morning and managed to get myself off of the bed without waking the man there beside me.

I found my clothes and got dressed as quickly as I could and was able to get out of the house without making any noise. Now I vaguely remembered the way that dad had driven me to this house and so set off to try and find my way home. It took me half an hour of walking to realize where I was and so it didn't take much longer to get home, and let myself in very quietly so as not to wake dad.

***

'You came home late last night,' dad said as he made breakfast for the both of us.

'Yes. I stopped for dinner, sorry,' I said as I sat down. 'I should have phoned you.'

'How did the cleaning go?' he asked as he sat down to start eating his breakfast.'

'Fine, just fine and he was that pleased that he said that he wouldn't mind me going back sometime as I'd done a good job,' I told him the lie, for I had enjoyed being fucked by him and having the other man's cock in my mouth and wouldn't mind another session, but cut out the drinking next time. I'm glad that he didn't ask at how much I'd been paid for I didn't know if he did or not, but on checking my purse later found a hundred dollar bill in there which wasn't there before. So I had been paid, but for what? Being a cleaner or a whore?

***

I was still going round to Mischelle's house for the monthly dinner and the sex between us that followed. The dinner as usual was good and the sex even better with us eating out each other's pussy as well as the sucking on our tits and nipples. We were both quite exhausted and I was lying on my back when Mischelle roused herself up and after kissing my tits, moved further up over my body so that she had her pussy directly above my face. She had her hands up on the wall behind the headboard and lowered her pussy down to my mouth to suck and tease her clit.

Then she peed in my mouth!

I tried to rise up but couldn't because her pussy was holding my head down as I coughed and nearly choked on her pee. I couldn't help but swallow some of it until I was able to close my mouth and had the rest flow over my face and chin. I even had to snort as some of it was going up my nose as I was trying to take in some air.

I finally managed to push her off of me when she stopped peeing and spluttered some of her pee back onto her face. 'Don't ever do that again!' I shouted at her, shaking my head so that more of her pee landed on her smiling face. 'You do that again, it'll be the last time you see me,' and I stormed off to the bathroom to wash my face and rinse out my mouth before returning to the bedroom.

'I'm sorry, Brooke. It…it just happened and I couldn't stop it. I really am sorry. You can pee on me if it'll make you feel better and forgive me,' she said. At least she had the right expression on her face as she apologized and so, with her open arms, I went into them for her to kiss me loads of times before going down and eating me out.

She never did it again and we stayed friends and lovers. Even though she did embarrass me later. That was that she wanted me to show her round the college I would be attending. It was a bright sunny day and I saw no problem with that and so I drove her towards the campus and as we entered the college grounds, she took off her top, baring her breasts. Boy, was my face red as I drove through the campus with her flashing her tits at all the guys we passed, some of them recognizing me and waving and cheering as I drove past.

'Did you have to do that, Mischelle?' I cried out as we left the campus. I couldn't have got out of there quicker than I did.

'Did you see their faces?' she laughed. 'They loved it as much as I did.'

'That's not the point! Most of those guys know me and I'm sure to get some flak from them later,' I cried.

'Loosen up, Brooke. The guys liked what they saw. You'll have all the boys after you with what you've got,' she smirked, giving my tits a brush with her hand. 'Pull over for a minute.'

'Why?'

'You'll see,' she said, so I pulled over and stopped and she handed me a camera. 'Take a couple of pictures of me as I am now.'

'You've gotta be joking!'

'Shut up and take some pictures,' she said leaning back against the door, smiling. I couldn't help but laugh and so took her picture. Well a couple at least before driving us back home as she put her top back on. I dropped her off at her house and drove on to stop and see Carli and asked her if she would like dinner at my house, and with a whisper, if she wanted to sleep over with it being our last night before going to college. She was all over me then and shouted out to her mom where she was going and didn't wait for an answer before closing the door and following me back to the car.

'What a lovely car, Brooke,' she said as I started the car with her stroking my leg. 'I wish my dad would buy me one.'

'You can't drive,' I said.

'Well I could learn to,' she pouted but kept on stroking my leg until I parked the car outside my house and we went inside. She helped me get dinner ready for when dad came home and not long before we had eaten and cleared the things away, told dad we were going to bed early as we had to be bright and breezy for our first day at college the next morning.

Up in my bedroom, Carli and I went into a clinch, our breasts being squashed between us as we kissed before taking each other's clothes off, kissing the flesh that was bared. We both took our time when we got onto the bed to take it in turns to kiss and suck on the upstanding nipple of each tit. We were both hungry to suck pussy and I had her go down on me first and loved to feel her tongue roving over my clit as well as diving in and out of my vagina. Such was my need for release, it wasn't long before I had my orgasm, flooding Carli's mouth making her splutter, but the good girl she is, swallowed it and kept on working on me. It wasn't long then before she moved up my body, kissing all the way up with a brief stop to kiss each nipple before kissing me on the lips.

We rolled over and I moved down, kissing her tits and sucking on them the same as she had done to me before carrying on and delving into her cave to bring her up to an orgasm for me to have the delight of making her come so soon for me to drink her dry. We made love again later with us being in the upside down position so that we could see to each other at the same time, it making it a change to be eating out her pussy at this different angle. We eventually fell asleep in each other's arms.

***

Both of us were awake early and had another session between us before getting out of bed and having a shower, both of us in the cubicle to wash each other, taking a long time in the doing so between our legs and breasts.

We cooked breakfast between us and dad had soon eaten his and after giving us both a kiss on the cheek and saying that he hoped we both would enjoy our first day at college before he went off to work.

'I hope we can both be in the same room at night,' Carli said as we washed and cleaned up the debris from breakfast, but it didn't come about, for I found that we were allocated different rooms. My roommates I found out were Aleena, who I've already mentioned at the beginning, and Sammy and Elaine. We were all of the same age and I vaguely remembered seeing both Sammy and Elaine at my last school where Aleena did not attend, but got to know her quite well.

If you've been to college yourself, you know the drill, so I won't bother with telling you all that goes on there. It was after supper, that's what they called our dinner, that us four girls donned nighties before going for a wash and teeth cleaning as well as having a pee before getting into our beds. They were envious when they saw my nightie for it was of sheer nylon and almost opaque for my body beneath it could clearly be seen whereas they had cotton ones.

Now I always slept naked in bed and they had another surprise when I took mine off before getting into my bed, all three of them looking at me as I did so.

'You've got a lovely body,' said Sammy as she nestled herself into her bed.

'And you've had your nipples pierced,' said Elaine just before turning out the light. Aleena hadn't said a word, her face slightly on the red side as she had got into her bed that was next to mine. We settled ourselves down for the night and it must have half an hour after the light had been put out that I heard Aleena softly sobbing in her bed. It was several minutes before I got out of bed and moved over and got into hers and put my arms round her and had her sobbing into my shoulder.

'First time away from home, Aleena?' I asked softly as I cuddled her.

'Yes,' was the muffled reply.

'Well don't worry or think of it with me holding you. I'll look after you,' I said, getting a nice warm glow in my belly as I stroked her back, her head slipping down for her cheek to press against the tit that was on that side. I'm quirky I know, for with her face on my breast, I shifted myself slightly so that my nipple brushed her lips and like a small child, they opened and took the nipple inside and began to suck on it. She kept on sucking for quite some time before she fell asleep and I then did the same.

I was still there when Sammy and Elaine woke up.

'Have you been in her bed all night?' Sammy asked, sitting up and asking me as she saw I was awake.

'Yes,' I said as I sat up, the sheet falling away to reveal my tits and I saw Elaine give a grin, but my movement in the bed woke up Aleena whose red face appeared above the sheet. 'She was crying so I comforted her and fell asleep.' Nothing more was said at the time as we got up, me having to put something on before going out for my shower along with the other girls who were on the same floor and from different rooms.

There in the showers I saw all the other girls naked and wondered how many tits and pussies that would be available for me to have fun with, though it only came down to three. I must say in all truth, that I had the best looking body of the lot of them and quite proudly let them see all of me in my glory. I really did show off by walking the whole length of the corridor naked on going back to my room. I'd set the tone and later, some of the other girls did the same. Only once did a teacher who happened to come into our section one morning admonished me for not being dressed but had no comeback when I mouthed the words 'fuck off' but couldn't say anything back for I had not spoken the words. She never came back in the mornings after that.

At lights out that night, I didn't wait for Aleena to start sobbing but got straight into her bed and put my arms round her.

'Would you like me to comfort you again,' I asked, giving her a hug.

'Yes please, Brooke,' she said in a shy voice and had no compunction from moving down the bed a little and taking my nipple into her mouth to suck on. It was the next night that I got her to take off her nightie and I went and sucked on her tit, though giving her more of what it was all about in tit sucking.

It wasn't long before I was in Elaine's bed where we took it in turns to suck and play with each other's nipples, much to the annoyance of Aleena. Especially when Sammy wanted her turn, though she was more aware of female sex than the other two and we soon were using our fingers on each other's clit as we sucked on a tit.

So it wasn't long before Sammy and Elaine would be in one bed together and me being in with Aleena. She was delighted when I started using my finger inside her pussy and over the moon when I finally went down and played with her there using both tongue and fingers to give her first ever orgasm. There was no stopping her after this wonderful experience as she told me afterwards. It wasn't long before I was doing the same with Elaine and Sammy, turning them into full blown lesbians and was told that they were delighted that I had been their room- mate. Aleena couldn't get enough of me and even enjoyed at eating my pussy and taking in all my orgasmic juices. I was then queen of our room and had the three of them hang round me for the rest of the time in college.

Carli tried to get one of her roommates to have sex but failed and so she finished up quite miserable at college though we did manage to have each other at odd times without being caught. Though she did in her second year there and at a party one night, they covered her face in lipstick and then took a picture of her standing there with slut written on her upper chest.

This didn't do her any good when it was posted up on the entrance board, but it was soon taken down by one of the professors and destroyed. But this wasn't taken until the following year, and it was now our Christmas break.

Dad was glad to see me as he said that it was lonely being on his own and having to cook his own meals, which was a lie for I found that he had found a new girlfriend who turned up the following day. Her name was Denise and what caught my eye was the fact that she owned one of the latest cars produced by B.M.W. Our introduction by dad was somewhat cool and I guessed that I was going to have trouble with her and wasn't wrong as it later turned out. Now somebody must have been speaking out of turn about my orientation, for when I gushed about her car and asked if I could have a drive in it, she pulled me to one side out of dad's hearing.

'I'll let you have a drive if you eat out my pussy,' she had said. Now who the fuck told her that I was a lesbian? That was a question that I couldn't answer, but with her knowing, agreed, for I really did want to drive that smashing car she had, but it wasn't until the following day.

She turned up after dad had gone to work and she really lauded it over me, saying that she was dad's latest lover but wanted to sample his step-daughter, me! I was almost dragged into my bedroom, she didn't want to use dad's bed. I was completely helpless with the way things were going so fast with her taking my clothes off so that I was naked before her and had her eyes running all over my body. She never even kissed me or touched my breasts before she stripped off and laid herself down on my bed.

'Okay, Brooke! Eat my pussy and you can have a drive in my car,' she said with a smirk instead of a welcoming smile. Seeing her open legs and that pussy there waiting for me was enough in spite of by going down on her would get me to driving her car. I dived in and gave her the best head that I could, soon bringing her up to an orgasm with my mouth, tongue and fingers and had her erupt in my mouth for me to taste, drink and swallow.

Mind you, to my mind it was worth it. To be able to drive that fabulous car round the town almost having an orgasm myself at the power that it had and of the thrill that it gave me. We had sex quite a few times with this being the carrot. She was more of a slut than I was and had me take quite a few pictures of her over that Christmas and during the next holiday break.

This being one of the first that she had me take of her on the bed, though she had me take some more when we were out in the garden where she would pose on the lounger and showing off with a dildo in her hand, one of many which follows.

She was more of a slut than I was in wanting many pictures of her playing with that rubber cock apart from those of her on my bed before I plated her. But I got to drive her car quite often so it was worth it.

Now for some reason or another one day during this Christmas break, I didn't go to the shop with Bernadette, but stayed at home and it was that day that I really found out that dad was bi-sexual. He didn't know that I was at home and because I was playing with myself at the time, didn't bother with letting him know. I'd just finished playing with Peter when I heard a strange voice downstairs and then dad's voice. I couldn't hear what was being said so I got off the bed and went out to the top of the staircase, but quickly slipped down so that I could not be seen but had a clear view of down below through the upright bars of the balustrade.

There was this man from U.P.S. leaning up against the wall in the hall downstairs and he had his cock out of his trousers and there was dad, down on his knees sucking on it. I was gob smacked at actually seeing my dad sucking on another man's cock. It couldn't have been the first time either for what the upright man then said.

'You're a great cocksucker, man. I just love coming here and having you suck on my dick and cumming in your mouth.' I watched in fascination at dad's head bobbing up and down on that man's cock, seeing it come out for him to lick all round the circumcised head.

'Well you always taste nice,' dad replied before taking the head of that big cock back into his mouth to suck as his hand worked on the shaft by rubbing it up and down in his hand as he sucked. Soon the man put his hands to dad's head and held it tight as he began to thrust his hips forward and have him give out a groan as he shot his load into dad's mouth. Dad seemed to enjoy this as he kept on sucking this big cock and had obviously swallowed the cum of that man before letting it slip out for him to lick all over the head before leaning back onto his heels as the man then put his now deflating cock back inside his trousers.

Dad then rose up and the two of them went into an embrace and they kissed each other for several minutes before breaking apart and the man then going off to the door and leaving. I shot back into my bedroom and quickly got Peter out and sucked like crazy on it but sadly, didn't have it cum in my mouth like dad had done to that man, though, wet as I was at having witnessed dad sucking on another man's cock, still had an orgasm which helped relieve the tension that had built up inside of me.

It wasn't long before I heard dad leave the house and after giving him time to be well away, went downstairs and into his office. Now I had played games quite often on his computer, but now I was scrolling through all that he had on there and it didn't take long to find that he had quite a lot of pictures of him having sex with other men. Him sucking on them and them sucking on him as well as being fucked by another man and of him shoving his cock up another man's ass. Some of the pictures had been taken here in this house and others must have been in somebody else's as I didn't recognize the lay out.

So this confirmed that not only was dad bi-sexual but also fucked lesbians too. Maybe mom had found out that he went with other men that made her leave, or was it because he was also fucking the lesbians that she had had sex with? What a conundrum! I then remembered an old saying of letting sleeping dogs lie, and so never said anything about what I had seen dad do or what was on his computer when he came home that evening for his dinner.

I went to the shop the following day but not until I had paid Chris a visit. I haven't mentioned her before, but she was a hairdresser that worked from home and the beauty of it was that it didn't cost money to have my hair done. That's cash I'm talking about, for the payment was made in kind. She did my hair for nothing if I went down to eat and suck on her pussy. Do you know that the whole neighborhood was inundated with whores, lesbians and gay men. Some of the whores being male too. Well, for a free hair-do was to eat out Chris, and this I did quite frequently. So much so that we became quite close, well close enough to want to have some pictures taken of her, just like the others. Were we all sluts?

She seemed to get a lot of thrills from a vibrator when she didn't have a customer like me to take the place of it in bringing her to an orgasm, but she was worth it even if her tits were nothing like mine in both size and appearance. Mind you, I shouldn't have really been surprised to find out how many female customers she had to give her sex in return for a hair do.

Christmas day was a wash out with having Denise with us and made no bones about how she was fucking with dad and somehow I got on the wrong side of her for I went to bed early so that she could be humped by dad without me around. It must have been about two in the morning that she woke me up by straddling me and having her pussy pushed down onto my face.

'Eat me out, cunt!' she slurred, mashing herself down onto me. It took an effort just to lift her enough for me to breathe and just as I was going to tongue her, she pissed on me instead. Shocked isn't really a strong enough word for how I felt and with some superhuman strength, managed to dislodge her from off of my face. She fell to one side laughing her head off as her piss was still spraying all over me and the bed sheets as she fell. But enough with most of my naked body beneath them, got my legs up and pushed her off onto the floor.

'Wassa matter, slut? Don't you like my pee? Your dad does,' she slurred and broke out in a laugh again as she rolled over onto her front and got up from the floor and staggered out of my room. I was fuming as I got out of bed and stripped the wet sheets off before going into the bathroom for a shower to clean myself up before remaking my bed.

'Fuck the pair of them,' I said to myself in the morning as I made my own breakfast. 'Let her do the cooking if they want to eat.' I even left my dirty plate for her to wash up as well as I went out and round to Carli's house. Her mom let me in, telling me that Carli was still in bed and didn't stop me from going upstairs to her room where I woke her up as I got undressed and into bed with her.

I don't know if her mom now knew that Carli was a lesbian or not, for she never entered her bedroom without being asked, so I knew that we wouldn't be disturbed as we went and sucked and ate each other out in the sixty nine position. So as I said, Christmas was a washout unlike New Year's Eve. Now that was good, for both Carli and myself went round to

Bernadette's place where there was going to be a party. Most were girls with a few boys there and we had a good time. I say good for when we'd seen the New Year in, the party turned into an orgy. Everybody stripped off and began having sex by fucking each other as much as we could. I even managed to take a picture of Bernadette being fucked by her own half brother. Well more than one for he fucked her twice and I even got a picture of her sucking on his cock.

I think I had five orgasms that night having a different girl see to me in our fashion while I gave the same amount of eating a pussy, though I can't remember now exactly all who I had gone down on, but it was a lovely fucking party all round. The bonus for me was it was me who went down and sucked at Bernadette after her brother had pulled out after cumming inside her and got to have his sperm as well as her juices both mixed up for me to pull out of her as I sucked. Two for the price of one! It was great!

What a mess we looked like in the morning when we finally woke up, some with hangovers and looking like death, others without hangovers but walking about like naked zombies, me being one of them. I was one of the lucky ones to have my shower early and so had hot water to wash and clean myself up from all the dried juices that covered my face and hair and so it was off to see Chris and eat her out to get my hair done.

But it was soon back to college and Aleena as well as Sammy and Elaine. The three of them now loving the nights we had in our room, fucking each other as we kept changing partners. Keeping this up until the time came round for our summer break having now been at college for a whole year. I looked even more radiant than before, so sex was a good thing for me. I even got Sammy to have a nipple pierced for her to have a ring there and I had my tongue done so that I could have a stud there.

I gave up working at the dress shop with Mischelle though I did go round to her house quite often for dinner and sex, leaving Denise to do the cooking for dad's meals for I had her twice more piss on me at night when she was drunk. Though this last time I really clobbered her for doing it and split her lip, so that slowed down her sucking on dad's cock for a while.

Then one morning, dad told me that Mr. Chevoski wanted me to give his house another clean. Now that would mean another hundred dollars as well as having sex with him again though this time I would pour out my own drinks. I duly went round and he let me in and gave me a kiss as soon as I was inside the door.

'My, my, Brooke,' he said after the kiss. 'You look more beautiful than the last time I saw you.' I didn't argue for I know he was right though it preened me up with him saying so. Thanking him for the compliment, I got to work on giving the house a damn good clean and had finished close on six o'clock. I was all hot and sweaty when I had finished and helped myself to a beer from the fridge in the kitchen.

'Will you be sharing the shower with me again?' I asked as I drank some of the beer, rubbing one of my tits as I spoke.

'It will be an honor, Brooke,' he smirked, giving the front of his trousers a rub. 'And afterwards?' he asked with a big grin on his face.

'Yes if you don't spike my drinks this time and forget about that other fellow,' I replied with a grin on my face now. At least his face turned a little red at me mentioning about the drinks being spiked.

'Okay, Brooke. Shall we shower then?' he asked, finishing his beer. So we went upstairs to the big bathroom that I had not long cleaned and now was about to make it a mess again. We stripped off in the bedroom, him now revealing that he had a hard on with his cock sticking straight out from his groin, and we had that shower. Him doing the washing of me and me doing the same to him, really taking my time when I had my hand on his cock and balls, making sure that they were all really clean. I hadn't sucked on him this time and we went into the bedroom and onto the bed where I got him to go down on me first and so had my first orgasm of the evening. I then went down on him, lying on his back with his truncheon up on his stomach which I took hold of and held it up for me to then suck on.

Boy, did I get a big mouthful or not when I had him cum in there. I had worked his shaft with my right hand and I sucked and gently chewed on the head of his cock until his sperm shot out in jerks and fill me before I swallowed it all and licked him clean afterwards. This was just the start as we then went back downstairs bollock naked for us both to prepare and cook dinner for the two of us.

He couldn't keep his eyes off my tits as we ate and it wasn't until we had our dessert did I see that he had a raging stalk on for I had poured some cream on the nipples of my tits and had him lick it off and then saw that he was up and hard with an erection that I poured some onto the head of his cock and sucked it off. But just enough to keep him erect for I wanted his big cock back up inside me, so back to the bedroom again we went. He even goosed me as we went up the stairs, his finger actually moving into my ass which made me jump by not expecting that probe in my asshole.

Again I made him go down on me first and give me an orgasm by using his tongue and fingers inside me, filling his mouth with my love juice, though he also wiped his mouth as he moved up my body to suck on my tits before kissing me. We kissed for several minutes with me feeling his throbbing cock being squashed between our stomachs before I opened my legs for him to ease his body up off of mine so that his cock could slip down between them and have it pushed up inside me. His Peter was better than mine for his throbbed and pulsated inside of vibrating and it moved much better as he moved it in and out of my cunt.

Such was the thrill of it being better than the vibrator, I soon reached my peak with him being able to hold back his own cumming until I began to buck underneath to his now forceful pushing himself into me that we then both had our orgasms at the same time. I would have liked to have had a picture of us two like this in the same way that I had taken the photo of Bernadette being fucked by her half brother, but there wasn't anybody else there to take one, mores the pity for I would have liked one to keep to remember that he was a good fucker. He even went down on me again only this time he was taking in his own sperm as well as my juices.

Sated, we lay on our backs, his hand stroking my lower chest and stomach before he started speaking.

'Did you know that your step-dad is bi-sexual?' was the opening line. 'That he likes sucking on another man's cock?'

'No,' I lied, even after having seen him suck on the U.P.S. man's cock and pictures of him on his computer.

'Well he does. I even got him to suck on mine,' he said.

'How? When?' I exclaimed as if this was news to me. Well it was really as I didn't know that the two of them had done this.

'It was when I went and bought this house, well, buying it really, for I held back half of the money until it had been cleaned properly. So on the final inspection I found that the previous owner had not done all that had been promised. Your step-dad was with me at the time and said he would see that it was done by having you come over to clean it properly.' He gave a sigh.

'Well I was really mad and said that I wouldn't sign off and pay the balance until I had some form of recompense. I wanted to humiliate someone for the house not being ready for me to occupy if, and well, your step-dad was there. How can I be of help in that, he asked, and that was it. I want my cock sucked, I told him. I'll get Brooke to do it,' he said. No, I said. I want it done now, immediately or I'll have my money back and you can keep the house. I pulled down the zipper of my trousers and pulled my cock out. I don't do that sort of thing,' he said, but his eyes were looking down at my throbbing cock, not at me, but at my cock as I pushed him down onto his knees and told him to suck on it.

'He kept on protesting but not very convincing, him still looking at my cock and when some pre cum started to ooze out of the eye of my cock, he gave his lips a lick and used his tongue to take it off the head and into his mouth. The next was that he had the almost the whole length of my cock in his mouth, sucking and chewing away like there was no tomorrow. I called him all kinds of names, cocksucker, faggot and the like which didn't seem to faze him as he kept on rubbing my cock with his hand as he sucked.

'He could really deep throat a cock which showed that he was used to sucking on a man's erection and he had no trouble in taking the gallon of cum that I shot into his mouth and had him swallow it and still carried on sucking me dry and licking the head when I finished cumming. It was one of the best sucks I'd ever been given and told him that I sometimes had a few friends over for poker and if he came too and sucked on them, we could probably get them to buy some houses.'

'And did he?' I asked, fascinated that dad would do this to Brad, this being Mr. Chevoski's first name and had told me to call him Brad on this second meeting.

'Of course. He came and played some hands and finished off the evening by sucking on all four of us and he seemed to enjoy it too,' he replied.

'Well I'm surprised that he did,' I said.

'No surprise really, for you see, I own the agency and am really his boss, so he guessed that his job was on the line if he didn't,' Brad said. 'I would like you to come over one night when we play for you to see him in action and also have his baby daughter see him sucking rampant cocks.'

On looking down the bed I saw that he gotten another erection at telling me of how he got dad to suck on not only this cock I could see and had, but others too. I stroked it with my hand and moved down the bed and lifted it up and began to suck on him.

'You're nearly as good as your step-dad,' he said as I sucked and teased the winking eye of his cock with my tongue. 'Now that would be something to see, you sucking on his cock here.'

Now having just heard of dad sucking on his cock had aroused me and I was quite wet between my thighs and even more so now at what he had suggested in me sucking on dad's cock with him watching.

'Enough sucking, Brooke, let us have a good fuck,' he said, pulling his cock out of my mouth. 'Doggie fashion,' he added, and so I rolled over and got up onto my knees as he too moved up and got behind me. With his hands on my hips and my pussy being so wet, he slid into me quite easily as he began to fuck me. He kept pulling right out and then back in again several times until he gave me a shock. That was because on one pulling out and instead of moving back inside my wet pussy, shoved his cock up into my ass. With his cock being covered in my juices gave it the lubrication it needed to enter me without any trouble, also the fact that I wasn't prepared for it so I was completely relaxed and my sphincter muscle didn't come into play until he was fully up in my ass.

This was a first for me and it wasn't that bad in being fucked this way though I would rather have had him in the right place. But to him, a hole was a hole and so he carried on fucking me up the ass and felt his cum spray the insides of my canal when he shot his load.

At least he had the decency to go and wash his cock after he had cum inside me instead of me sucking him off if he'd been inside my pussy. He made up for fucking me up the ass by going down on me when he returned to the bed and gave me my orgasm that was a relief for my body. We kissed some more afterwards and I finished spending the whole night in his bed and had him fuck me again in the morning.

He kissed me goodbye as he gave me my money earned from the house cleaning and got me to promise to visit him at the next poker session when dad would be there too. I got wet even thinking about it on the way home and soon went round to see Bernadette and have her pussy to eat out and have her do the same to me.

***

What a surprise dad got when I walked in to the poker game two weeks later.

'What the hell are you doing here?' he cried out at seeing me enter the room.

'I was invited the same as you were,' I said, getting a funny feeling in my body at actually being there in the room with four other guys, Brad being one of them. 'Brad told me that you were gay, though I lied to him when I said that I didn't know, for I have for some time now and I want to see you sucking on an erect cock, something that I like doing too.'

'You can't!' he protested.

'Oh yes she will,' said Brad, his voice carrying a threat in the tone he used. I saw the defeat in dad's eyes as he knew that what the boss wanted, he got. So it wasn't long before Brad sprawled himself on the sofa with his legs open and with his rampant cock out and dad, with a sheepish look at me, went down onto his knees and sucked off his boss. Christ! I was creaming my panties at seeing him take the whole length of that cock deep into his throat in the process of sucking on Brad. Then he sucked on the other three men there and one even took a picture of him as he licked the big cock that the man had. A copy that was later given to me which I've kept as a memento.

The icing on the cake if it could be called that was when dad was told to get his own cock out for me to suck on. Dad was unhappy at being told to do this, but he reluctantly got his own cock out from his trousers and showed that in spite of me being his step daughter, he had an erection in anticipation of himself being sucked, and sat down on the sofa.

I got down onto my knees and went between his open legs and saw the pain in his eyes that his daughter was going to suck his cock in front of four other men. I gave my lips a lick and bent my head down and took the head of his cock into my mouth and gave him the best blow job that I could. Why it's called a blow job when all you do most of the time is suck it, I'll never know. But suck it I did and had him give out a groan as I did so and then another big one when he finally erupted in my mouth, filling it with his seed. Boy was I wet in my panties at doing this and swallowing his cum when he'd finished.

I sat back on my heels when I'd finished licking the head of his cock clean and watched him putting it away inside his trousers, him not looking at me as he did so. I then had a wicked thought at seeing that Brad had his cock out of his trousers again and it was up and hard sticking out in front of him. I got up and took off my skirt and panties and went and laid down the sofa after dad had got up from it and beckoned to Brad.

The pity was that I couldn't see the expression on dad's face as he watched as Brad came over and got between my legs and pushed his cock up into me and fucked me. What with him watching me suck on my step-dad as he called him, it had really aroused him and it didn't take but a few minutes of him fucking me before he shot his load of cum into me.

Needless to say that dad didn't speak to me for a week and I think he was glad when I returned to college. In a way I was glad to be back with Aleena, Sammy and Elaine for us to have our nightly sessions of sex which we all enjoyed. We are half way through this term now and all doing well in the courses we are taking with me taking time off as it were from my studies to be writing this story of my life so far. I'm still here in the library as I have now brought you up to date of my life so far and Aleena is creaming her panties as she can't wait to read this mini manuscript. So I hope you have enjoyed it as much as I have had in the writing and having Brooke revealed.

~~The End~~

Here is a sample from another story you may enjoy:

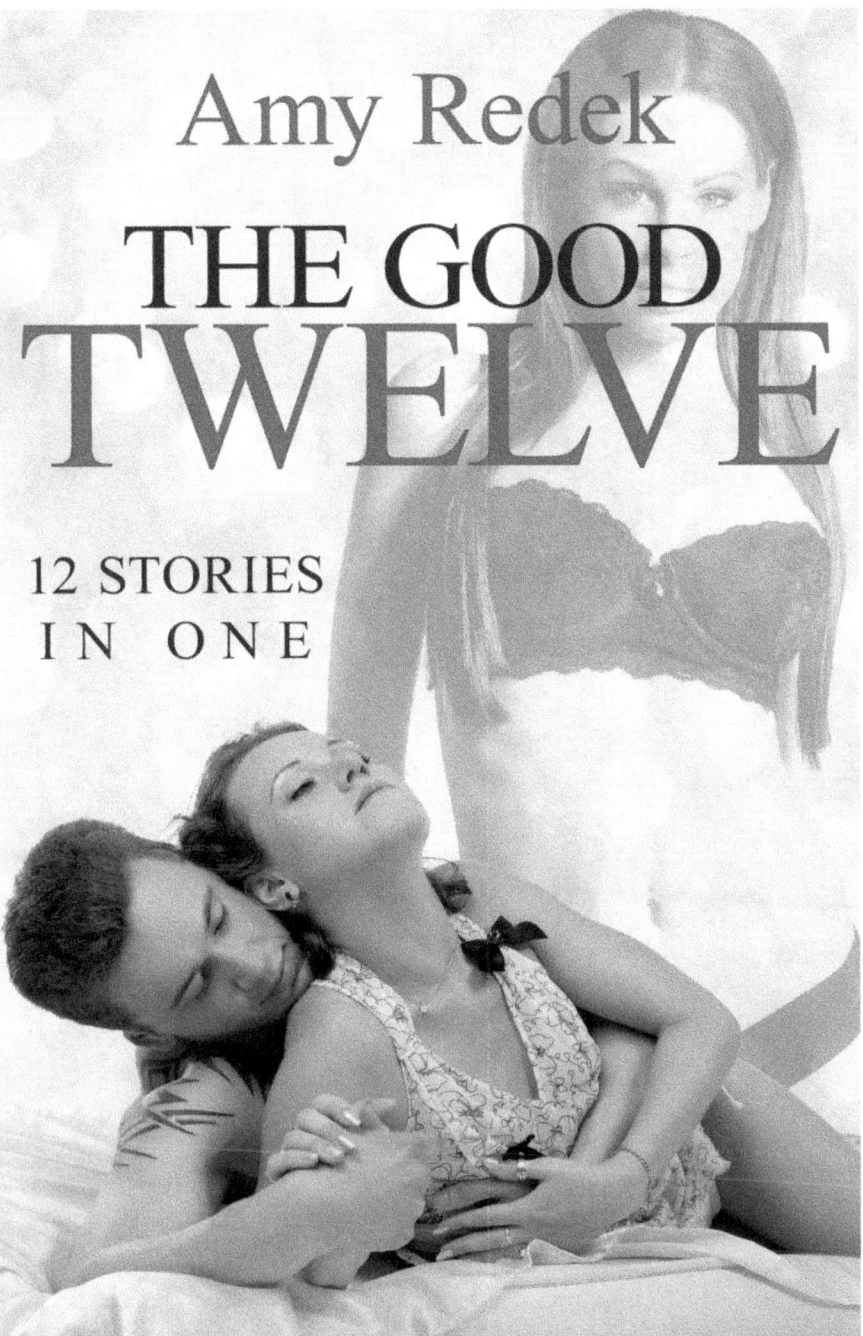

Amy Redek

THE GOOD
TWELVE

12 STORIES
IN ONE

My father passed away about a year ago and so I was now alone in my house for my mother had walked out from us many years ago when I was only a child of five. The reason for that my father told me later, was because of him being caught getting another woman pregnant. After an awful row, she had left us, leaving father to raise me on his own.

It was disappointing not to have my mother around but he looked after me well enough in seeing that I was brought up properly. He often took me fishing on the river that ran past the bottom of our garden where we had a boathouse that held our small boat. I say boathouse though it was not a proper one but more of a large shed that covered a small inlet into our garden.

The river was called the Pax and our house was on the outskirts of the town of Paxham, having taken its name from the river when it was just a small hamlet. The boat, which I never did know what type it should be called, was quite deep in the middle and had a small outboard motor attached. I liked this boat because of the inside depth of it for when I took my girlfriend out in it for fishing, it was easy for us to lie down in the bottom of it for us to kiss and cuddle and not be seen when anchored out in the middle of the river.

There was one particular spot about a mile and a half down river where for a stretch of at least fifty yards on either bank, gorse bushes came right down to the river's edge and so it was unlikely that persons on the banks could get down to the river and see my boat anchored and us kissing there.

On this particular day, I was now twenty-six years of age and my girlfriend, Josie, was twenty-one. I loved our kissing of each other and found the courage to ask if she would marry me. I was over the moon when she said yes. I then saw that it was time to return to our houses and so began to pull up the small light anchor that had held the boat still in the slowly moving river.

'It's caught on something,' I said, having difficulty in upping the anchor and she moved to the bow to give me a hand. With both of us pulling on the anchor's rope, it slowly began to come up but we didn't get it out of the river. For as we slowly gathered the rope in we found what it had caught and Josie gave out a scream and we both let go of the rope to sink back down with what the anchor had attached itself to, for we had seen the head of a skeleton!

'Christ Almighty,' I had exclaimed, turning round to hold a shaking Josie and calm her down at her having seen what had once been a living person. What I then did was to get the empty bottle of water he still had in the boat and tied this to the anchor rope that I had cut free and let it float on top of the water to show where this skeleton was.

It was a silent pair that was in the boat as I got the engine running and moved it back upstream to my house where, after mooring the boat, phoned the police to tell them of what we had found. About an hour later, I was being interviewed by two police officers, one of them being a woman, and knew both of them as they were locals like me. They said that after they had got hold of a diver and a boat, they would collect me to show them where in the river I had anchored, which they did.

So with them collecting me, and with their boat being more powerful than mine, we're soon down where I had anchored and found the floating bottle. Now the diver went over the side and two minutes later was back up and confirmed that there was indeed a skeleton anchored below by what looked like a roadside grating. This was confirmed after they had recovered the remains of which I had no part for they had left me behind when they did this later in the day, but was told of this the following day when I gave a full statement down at the local nick.

Two divers had gone down, one to lift the skeleton and one the grating that was chained to the legs. Between them, they got both to the surface where others took over to get them into the boat where they were taken to the town for an autopsy. I queried this word asking how can you do an autopsy on a skeleton? I thought that it had to have flesh for this to be carried out but was told that bones could still be identified by any bone marrow left, the pelvic bones and teeth. They guessed that it could be somebody local for the grating was of the same style as that used in the town to drain off the rain water from the roads.

Well the pelvic bones told them that it was of a female and they could also start checking with the teeth because of the possibility of it being a local woman and these teeth being noted at some dentist's records. It took a few weeks but they found a match which shocked me, for the woman's name was Joan Redmond. I haven't told you yet that my name is Jack Redmond and this was most likely the bones of my mother that I had hooked onto.

I was in shock!

Could this really have been my mother who was supposed to have walked out from our home twenty one years ago? There was only one way to find out and agreed for them to do a D.N.A. test on me to see if it was a match to the bones of the woman. This didn't take long to confirm that there was a match and it was indeed that of my mother.

Now this raised another question, apart from the fact that my father must have murdered her, though how, they couldn't say, and chained her legs to the grating and dumped her there and put out the story that she had left him because of him getting another woman pregnant. When the news broke out in the town, the question came from the mother of Josie who claimed that it was my father, John Redmond who had gotten her pregnant and therefore requested that Josie went through D.N.A. testing to compare it with mine.

If you enjoyed this sample then look for **The Good Twelve**.

The Painted Sword

Cruise Control

Wild Pleasures

Lending My Beloved

Lady of Cuckolds

Lady of Pleasure

Lady Magenta

Sexually Overdosed

Meeting My Fancy Dear

Prison Sex Slave

Chasing A Shadow

The Hostel

The Island

Thirst for Drugs and Pleasure

Forgotten Identity

Grey Memories

Chronos: Time Machine

The Hard Bomber

Honeymoon Abduction

The Yacht Sins

Summer at the Villa

Practice Makes Perfect

Stranger Danger

Following Father's Footsteps

The Square Circle

The Wizard of Kos

Coming Together

Out in the Real World

Me, Carol and Raoul

Under the Mistletoe

Play House

A Cocktale for Sherry

Loving Rhett

Farell

Homos Ubique

Foxhole

Deaf, Dumb and Blind

Loving the Mechanic

Up for Sale

No White Snow

Love Motel

A Man's Toy

Three for One

The Sex Brigade

The Good Twelve

His Special Lessons

Love and Lust

***

I REALLY LOVE Reviews!

If you enjoyed this book, please share the love and don't forget to leave a review on Amazon or the site of any other retailer you purchased this book from!

I highly appreciate your reviews, and it only takes a minute to write & post one. I can't tell you how much this means to me!

You'll find the list of all my books on my Author Central page... just in case you'd like to leave a review for other books of mine you've read but didn't have time to leave a review.

*Amazon Author Central – http://www.amazon.com/Amy-Redek/e/B00A48NQ72

One Last Thing, For Kindle Readers...

When you turn the page, Kindle will give you the opportunity to rate this book and share your thoughts on Facebook and Twitter. If you enjoyed my writings, would you please take a few seconds to let your friends know about it? Because... when they enjoy they will be grateful to you and so will I.

Thank You!

Amy Redek
amy_redek@awesomeauthors.org

About the Author

George Eliot was a famous writer, though at the time, only male authors were recognised. It was in fact the pen name of Mary Ann Evans, a female.

When I started writing, I thought that if a woman could use a male name, why, with me being male, why couldn't I use the name of a female? Though to be different, I made my writer's name from an anagram of my real name.

I wasn't the brightest spark in my school days and it was only while being in the Merchant Navy did I self-educate myself. That being mostly literature, classical music and artists, like Tolstoy, Chopin and Rembrandt. After leaving the navy, I had several jobs, finishing up by being a working boss using my own maxim that 'Management is the art of delegation.'

It's when I became self-employed that I began to write, though sadly, not many of my books can be published because of certain laws that forbid certain aspects of life. This never fazed me for I was really writing just to please myself having a wide range of the human psych.

Having written ninety stories, my only aim now is to reach one hundred. I give thanks to the publishers for at least putting some of my efforts out for others to enjoy as much as I did in the writing of them.

You may also like the books by these authors:

JACK
RYDER

e-MAIL
ORDER
BRIDE

Transgender
Romance

Seatac was a mad house at 9pm on a Friday night. I was glad that I had left early so I had plenty of time to deal with the sports traffic on I-5 due to the Mariners Game. Then I had to deal with the security checks to make my way to the proper air terminal gate for Sam's arrival. I made it to the gate with ten minutes to spare. I felt an overwhelming giddiness as I watched her airplane pull up to the loading dock.

"Ooooh, Fuck me," I gasped beneath my breath as I saw her coming down the ramp. She was wearing a white tube dress that fit her like a second skin. It was so short that I could see the bottom inch of her white panties as she walked towards me. She was wearing a big round black hat and her long black hair was in a tight braided ponytail. She had huge dark sunglasses on and was smiling broadly as she got closer and closer. Her long muscular legs looked fabulous.

"You are even more gorgeous in person," she told me in that wonderfully husky voice as she bent forward to kiss one cheek and then the other.

"Oh Sam...You look gorgeous," I groaned my reply. It thrilled me to see all the heads turning as we made our way to the baggage claim to get her luggage. And even more when she reached down to hold my hand as we waited at the turnstile.

"Ha-ha-ha-ha, I should have guessed that you would have a Hummer," Sam giggled when I pointed out my forest green Humvee.

"It was my divorce present to myself," I informed her as I opened the passenger door. "And my cabin in the hills was the other." My dick wiggled as she swung her legs into the vehicle. I got a quick glance of her white panties and a great look down the top of her dress at her tits. Her nipples were just as hard as last night.

"I have something to tell you before we get to the hotel." She said it very softly as we were pulling out of the parking garage. "I make porn movies, Bobby...I am a porn Queen in Russia."

I glanced over at her and she was gazing at me intently. "Wow, Sam...How did I ever get so lucky?" My voice sort of trembled a bit. "I'm even more amazed that you have an interest in me now."

I felt her hand rest gently on my thigh as I turned my attention back to driving the vehicle. "I think that I may be the lucky one," she whispered it softly. "I came here to see you because there is something I need to show you." She said it so softly that I could barely hear her. "I have a feeling about you...that it will be okay." Her hand gently brushed up and down my thigh. I could feel my dick throbbing in my jeans. "You have no idea how much I hope I am right," she added.

I couldn't keep my eyes off of Sam while she was checking in at the hotel. Neither could any of the other men in the front lobby area. By the time we made it to the elevator, several of the bell hops and a couple of the men from the lobby had asked Sam for her autograph. Except they knew her by the name Samantha Bone.

I could tell that Sam was a bit annoyed and upset as the elevator started to rise towards the penthouse suite. "It bothers me that all those men knew who I am and have seen me naked," she whispered it softly. "But you haven't yet." She sort of hung her head as she finished.

I reached over and held her hand gently. "I'm sure that whatever you are worrying about will be okay," I told her as I squeezed her hand. "I've been told that I am a fairly progressive sort of man." I chuckled.

Sam turned to face me and gave me a half smile. "I certainly hope you are, Hun," she answered me.

As soon as were in the penthouse suite, Sam kicked off her white heels and tossed her black hat onto the easy chair near the kitchen. She sat her sunglasses on the counter then reached up to grab a bottle of vodka from the top cabinet.

"Oh Geezus," I gasped as I gazed at her ass sticking out under her tight dress as it pulled up in back.

Sam poured the vodka into two 4 oz. tumblers then carried them and the bottle back into the living room. "Sit on the couch and be comfortable," she told me as she handed me one of the drinks. After she slammed down her entire drink, she pointed to mine. "Bottoms up...Hun," she giggled. As soon as I swallowed mine down, she refilled both tumblers and then stepped back about two feet from the couch.

"Moment of truth," she chuckled softly. Standing directly in front of me, she slowly pulled down the top of her tight dress until her tits were fully exposed to me. "Oooh Sam," I gasped. I could feel my pecker swelling in my jeans as I glanced at her gorgeous tits.

"The reason I didn't tell you about the porn movies is that I was afraid that you might ask me what sort of porn." She said it as she wiggled her dress down to her feet and kicked it off. I could now see that she wasn't wearing white panties, it was a white bikini bottom.

"You are so gorgeous, Sam," I moaned as I gawked at her beautiful body.

"Yes...but you haven't seen all of me yet," she whispered as she pulled the strings on her bikini and it fell off.

What she had on underneath the bikini I had never seen before. It was like a thong. But not quite a thong. It was a small fabric cup sort of thing with a thong strap in the center that went up the crack of her ass. There was a thick string that wrapped around her waist and tied to the center fabric in back. "This is what you haven't seen," she said it timidly as she reached behind to untie the string.

As the tiny cup fell to the floor, I was stunned and exhilarated at the same instant. My eyes were riveted between her legs at the perfect six inch flaccid cock. "Ooooh Sam," I whispered. "That is so...extraordinary." I could feel my dick throbbing.

"It's....okay?" Sam cooed as her eyes lifted up to peer into mine.

"Oh Sam, it's better than okay...it is...wonderful! I want to feel it get hard in my hand this first time," I whispered as I reached forward to gently fondle her perfect six inch dick...

If you enjoyed this sample then look for **E-Mail Order Bride** by **Jack Ryder.**

Nicki Homewood

The Debtor's Performance

Exhibitionist Erotica

I sat at the table and prayed for a number higher than eight. The dice felt warm in my sweaty hand and I could feel my heart pounding in my chest. They rolled round inside my hand and I scattered them down the table, closing my eyes at the final moment of ejection as they made their way down the table and settled.

I let my head fall backwards, tried to relax my neck, feeling my rich golden hair fall down my back, hoping against hope that finally my luck had changed. I heard the girl next to me gasp and I tried to determine what that meant for me. Had I won at last?

Three and Two.

Not enough, not nearly enough.

What would happen next, I wondered. I was so far beyond the limit of credit that I had initially agreed that I could not believe they would let me borrow more. My credit cards were already maxed out and however good a customer I was, I couldn't believe that they would let me keep on playing. I had already had an interview with Mr Abadlioi last week after the previous set of losses.

I looked down at the beautiful blue satin dress that I was wearing. I had picked it out because the last time I had worn it, I had been lucky, had come away better than level. I loved the big slit down the front, the way that it showed off so much of my cleavage. Around the casino there were certain rules of behaviour that I loved. Guys could admire a beautiful woman and women could be admired, but no one would make much of a move, no one would hassle you. It was nice, and safe.

Economically it was not safe, I reflected. Economically it was a disaster, a life-changing, misery-inducing, marriage-destroying disaster.

I could feel my string pulling into my ass a little, the tops of my stockings on my hips, the lace gently hugging me to keep themselves in place. The satin was smooth and sexy against my skin and I thought that I may never be able to afford to buy such a garment again.

Silence descended over the table as behind me I could hear a group of people approaching me. I turned slowly with a forced smile on my lips.

"Mrs DiAngelo, perhaps I could suggest that you come this way," Mr Abadlioi asked, a cold politeness still evident in his voice.

Behind him were two guys, not goons exactly but big guys that could look after themselves in a fight I was sure. Not that fighting was exactly my thing.

We walked away from the table and I could feel the eyes of all the people on the floor track me as I walked out past the tables, past the fruit machines and down a darker corridor leading to the backrooms where the reality of casino debts started to encroach on real life. No longer here were you just dealing in coloured plastic chips, this was where cheques and credit cards lived, and debt collectors and lawyers I supposed.

The guys on either side of me didn't even look at me. Here I was wearing a practically skin tight satin dress, pulled tight over my tits, accentuating my 34B breasts that were otherwise unencumbered with cover or support. I knew that men found this dress very sexy. I had seen the looks of lust, of desire in their eyes many times. I knew that my husband loved to see me in it, loved to see the way it showed the lines of my firm breasts, and just gave away a little of my nipples as they pressed into the fabric.

I was shown once again into his office and sat down opposite him, ensconced behind his huge solid oak desk. He smiled at me graciously.

"Well, Mrs DiAngelo, we seem to find ourselves here again. Well, well, well. And so soon," he started.

"I seem to be going through a very unlucky run," I mumbled nervously.

"Yes, well that is certainly clear. But the problem for me is now really just how we are going to recover the funds. I seem to remember last time that you were very keen to keep it between the two of us. Does that remain the case?" he asked, his eyes roaming down over my form.

If you enjoyed this sample then look for **The Debtor's Performance** by **Nicki Homewood.**

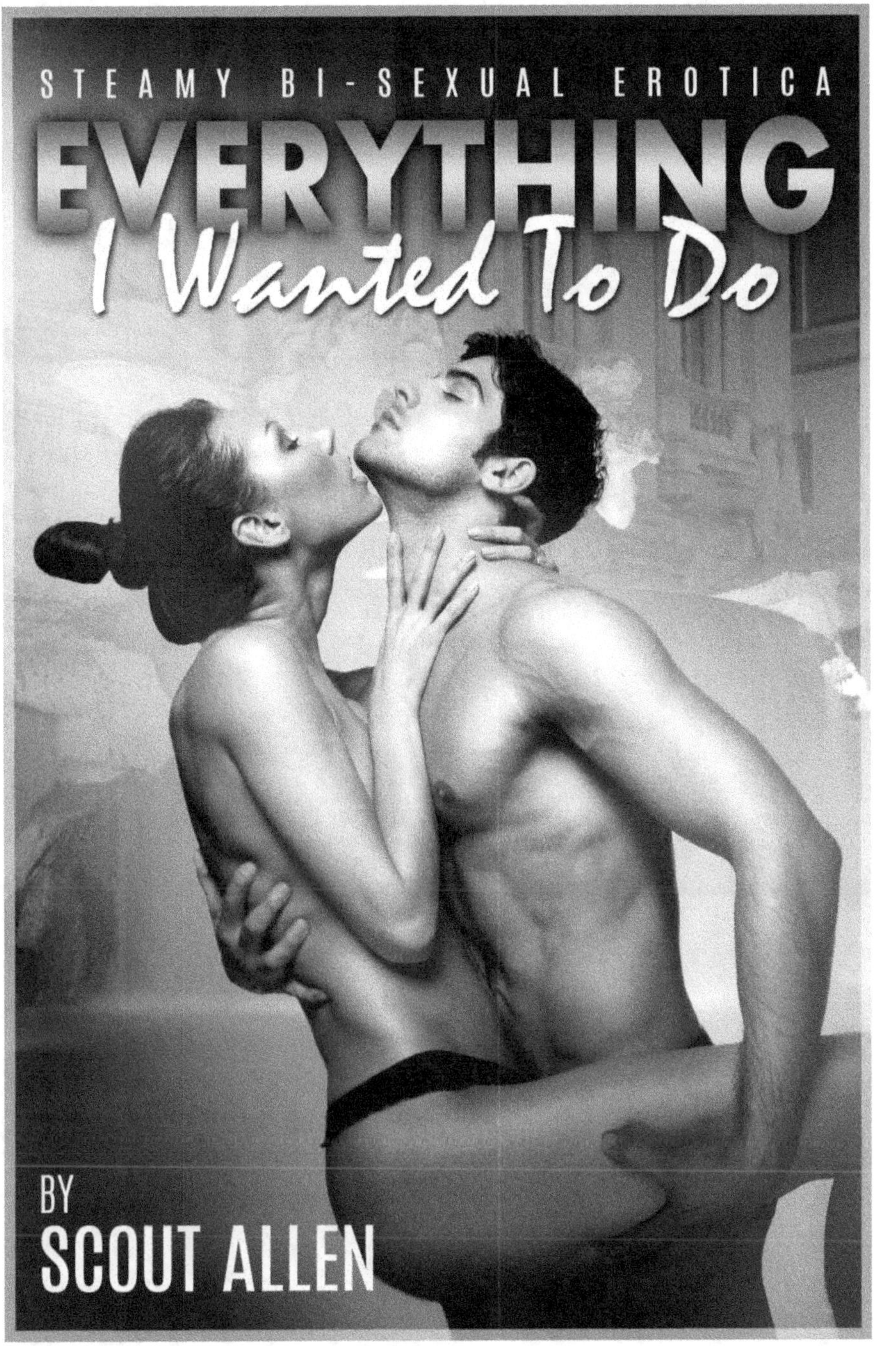
STEAMY BI-SEXUAL EROTICA
EVERYTHING
I Wanted To Do
BY
SCOUT ALLEN

"Did you ever think we'd be doing this?" she asked as she pulled off her shirt and unbuckled her pants.

"Yeah but not without getting arrested," I commented while I slipped off my pants and pulled off my shirt.

We were in the country of Italy, Rome more specifically, at the fountain of Trevi. You know that large fountain with statues of horses and Italian people, large water out front and sprayers?

Anyway, I and my friend had been doing the whole backpacking through Europe thing when the Disappearance happened.

"Hey what are you doing?" I asked as she was pulling down her panties.

"What? If I'm going to go swimming in Rome's world famous Trevi fountain, I'm going to do it naked," then she pulled off her bra and looked at me. "Aren't you?"

Samantha wasn't a curvy goddess but she was pretty. Five foot six, B-cup breasts, bright red hair, blue eyes just bright enough to catch the eye, slim but not starvingly so, with slight hips that go down to a strip of hair leading to her otherwise bare sex. She was the most beautiful woman I'd seen in ages.

"Julian?" she said as I checked her out, her not shy in the least.

"Oh yeah," and I quickly stripped out of my shorts.

Climbing over the stone edge, we began our swimming around, thankfully because my penis had become erect.

"I wonder where they all went," she mused for what seemed like the hundredth time.

"Who knows," I added.

Not three days ago, the world seemed to have enough of the people's bullshit and it seemed like everyone else was just…gone. No clothing left over, no corpses to clean up, no crashes of cars. Time seemed to stop for everyone. And then when it was back, we were alone.

Thinking to myself, I wondered where everyone was, what they were doing, how we were missed in it all.

Something touched my skin and I fumbled and partially drowned myself before coming up for air. Sam was laughing out loud and standing on her feet, her bare breasts jiggling as she laughed.

I was now painfully erect.

"Why you.." and I tackled her back into the water as we wrestled and splashed until we ended up against one statue with my back pressed against the wall and her pressed against me.

We were both panting from the exertion. Her bare skin pressed against mine, her breasts pressed against my chest as she looked into my eyes. My painfully erect penis pressed against her warm crotch. Something came to mind but I decided not to say it. Instead, I simply moved my hands down to her ass and gripped it.

We'd been alone together for three days, no sex for weeks for either of us. We were young, horny, and willing.

I kissed her and she kissed me back.

Pulling her ass so her lips where pressed against my cock, her soft skin in my hands as her hands roamed over my chest and skin sending ripples of pleasure through my body. She was hungry, lustful… so was I…

If you enjoyed this sample then look for **Everything I Wanted To Do** by **Scout Allen.**

Gideon Elliot

The Good Bitch

Surprising Erotic Discovery

BDSM Erotica

She knew that if she wasn't there when he got back from the garage, he didn't like it.

"I'm an old-fashioned kinda guy," he explained one night after he'd smacked her around because dinner wasn't ready when he got home and the house was a mess. He'd had a long and hard day, and sometimes a guy loses his temper. He wouldn't be normal if he didn't.

"I mean, I work all day to support us, and all you gotta do, I mean all you gotta do is keep up your end of the bargain, right? I mean that's what you wanted, wasn't it? Just when I come home, my slippers are out and there's a hot meal ready, and the house is a place I can be proud to say I live in. And if you fix yourself up a little, try to look a little pretty, hey, that's icing on the cake. You know what I'm sayin'?"

"I do, Larry; you're right. I'm sorry."

"I know you are," he said, taking her in his arms. "What am I gonna do with you?"

"I'll get better, Larry. I mean it. I want to."

She was looking up at him, now, wishing he would kiss her, and he did. A frisson of electricity passed through her and her body fell limp against his.

"That's it, baby. Papa's home," he said and he slid his hand down her back beneath her cutaway jeans and started circling and teasing her budding aureole and then plunged in. She gasped. Her eyes glazed over.

* * *

He threw her onto the bed spread eagle, face down, and pinned her there with the might of his arms and knees.

"Tell me what you want me to do."

"I want you to fuck me."

"Tell me where."

"In my pussy."

"Where?"

"Up my pussy."

He circled her wrists with his fists and pulled her arms back. She felt as if her shoulder blades were cracking.

"Where?"

"Up my pussy," she repeated beginning to whimper.

He pulled her arms more. She began to sob.

"Where do you want me to fuck you, bitch?"

"In my pussy," she cried.

"Where?"

The pain was becoming excruciating.

"Up my ass."

"Again."

"Up my ass."

"Because I'm a pig."

"Ask for it, pig."

"Please fuck me up the ass."

"Beg."

The pain was intense.

"Please, Larry."

"Please what?"

"Please fuck me?"

"Where?"

"Please fuck my ass. Oh, please fuck my ass. Fuck my ass."

His cock was like a dagger poking at her now, and his breathing was wet with spittle on her neck as he tore into her flesh with his teeth.

"Tell me why."

"Because I'm a shitty, worthless little bitch and need to get fucked up the ass."

He ploughed into her. She screamed until the pain crashed like lightning, and then everything caught and turned upside down as in an inverting mirror and the pain turned to an ecstasy of pleasure she had forgotten, and she screamed as he stabbed her repeatedly, fucking her ass and digging his fingers into her arm pits and grabbing her breasts in fistfuls and scratching her nipples with his calloused finger tips until he collapsed on top of her and she almost couldn't breathe.

"You're gonna feel that all day tomorrow," he crowed, "and you're gonna know for sure whose bitch you are."

If you enjoyed this sample then look for **The Good Bitch by Gideon Elliot.**

"Jack, Gloria would like to see you in her office."

It was the one thing that no one at Stearns Inc. wanted to hear because it usually meant that you were history. Gloria Stearns believed that she owed it to the people getting bad news to get it from her direct and not from some lower minion. The current economy sucked and Stearns was downsizing and it looked like I was on my way to the unemployment line.

I knocked on the door to Gloria's private office and heard her say "Come in." I opened the door and stepped into her office as she came out from behind the desk and walked toward me with her hand out-stretched in greeting. I felt the same tingle in my groin that I got every time I saw her. Tall, willowy and with runway model good looks she lit any number of fires as she walked through the office. I took her hand as she said, "Jack, how nice to see you. Have a seat."

After shaking hands she moved back behind the desk and sat down. As I took a seat she picked up a folder on her desk, glanced through it quickly, looked up at me and then back down at what I could only assume was a file on me.

"How long have you been here at Stearns Jack?"

"Eleven years. I came to work for your father right out of high school."

"It must have been hard for you to work here full time while going to college at night."

"It wasn't easy Miss Stearns, but your father helped me a lot."

"Yes, I know. For some reason he never explained why he looked on you almost as a son. He even loaned you the money for your education and then forgave the loan as a graduation present. Why did he do that Jack?"

"I don't know."

"Yes you do Jack, and what's more, so do I. Why did you do it Jack? Why did you stick your neck out like that?"

"Your father was a good man Miss Stearns and I wasn't about to let that bitch screw up your father's

If you enjoyed this sample then look for **Bought And Used** by **Just Plain Bob.**

WANT FREE COPIES OF MY BOOKS?
Just visit my blog and download free copies of my books:
amy-redek.awesomeauthors.org/amy-redek